This is how  lives, but th same

The Executioner pushed the thought from his mind.

Santos followed Bolan closely, turning frequently to check the corridor behind them for approaching enemies. He caught her movements from the corner of his eye and reckoned she was doing all that could be done. The hotel was a warren built as if with ambushes in mind and there was no way he could protect them from all sides.

No way at all.

That was the price of hunting lethal predators. Sometimes—more times than he could count, in fact—the hunter was transformed into the prey.

Like now? he wondered.

He wasn't sure, but Bolan knew one thing beyond a shadow of doubt—he wasn't giving up. If he could swap his own life for a thousand hostages, he'd reckon it was a decent trade.

MACK BOLAN ®
The Executioner

The Don Pendleton's
Executioner®
FINAL RESORT

A GOLD EAGLE BOOK FROM
W❂RLDWIDE®

TORONTO • NEW YORK • LONDON
AMSTERDAM • PARIS • SYDNEY • HAMBURG
STOCKHOLM • ATHENS • TOKYO • MILAN
MADRID • WARSAW • BUDAPEST • AUCKLAND

First edition December 2008

ISBN-13: 978-0-373-64361-5
ISBN-10:   0-373-64361-6

Special thanks and acknowledgment to
Michael Newton for his contribution to this work.

FINAL RESORT

Printed in U.S.A.

War is cruelty, and you cannot refine it.
>—General William T. Sherman,
>1820–1891

No honest soldier has anything good to say about war—but we fight where we can, where we must.
>—Mack Bolan

THE
MACK BOLAN

LEGEND

Nothing less than a war could have fashioned the destiny of the man called Mack Bolan. Bolan earned the Executioner title in the jungle hell of Vietnam.

But this soldier also wore another name—Sergeant Mercy. He was so tagged because of the compassion he showed to wounded comrades-in-arms and Vietnamese civilians.

Mack Bolan's second tour of duty ended prematurely when he was given emergency leave to return home and bury his family, victims of the Mob. Then he declared a one-man war against the Mafia.

He confronted the Families head-on from coast to coast, and soon a hope of victory began to appear. But Bolan had broken society's every rule. That same society started gunning for this elusive warrior—to no avail.

So Bolan was offered amnesty to work within the system against terrorism. This time, as an employee of Uncle Sam, Bolan became Colonel John Phoenix. With a command center at Stony Man Farm in Virginia, he and his new allies—Able Team and Phoenix Force—waged relentless war on a new adversary: the KGB.

But when his one true love, April Rose, died at the hands of the Soviet terror machine, Bolan severed all ties with Establishment authority.

Now, after a lengthy lone-wolf struggle and much soul-searching, the Executioner has agreed to enter an "arm's-length" alliance with his government once more, reserving the right to pursue personal missions in his Everlasting War.

Prologue

Guantanamo Bay, Cuba

The first explosion stunned Lance Corporal Kenneth Pyle. Patrol duty at Gitmo was strictly routine, no surprises encouraged, since Camp X-Ray had been established to contain leading terrorists, insurgents, or whatever the hell they were labeled this week.

The enemy, Pyle thought, and let it go at that.

So, no surprises in the guise of training measures for Marines who drew guard duty at the camp, in case somebody had an itchy trigger finger and he greased a drill instructor.

But what in hell was *this* about?

The first blast sounded like a half-pound charge of C-4 or the equivalent. It echoed from the east side of the camp, meaning that Pyle could not investigate despite his shock and sudden, urgent curiosity. The first rule of guard duty in the Corps was to stay alert and man the post assigned, no matter what distractions surfaced in the course of any given shift. Pyle couldn't leave his beat along the camp's northern perimeter unless directly ordered by the Sergeant of the Guard or someone who outranked him.

Pyle was thinking accident when two more high-explosive detonations rocked the base, one on the southern side, and one— unless Pyle missed his guess—not far from the command post.

And it wasn't any goddamned accident.

He knew that, now.

Pyle jacked a round into the chamber of his M-16 and watched the wire, remembering the orders that had been drilled into him from day one of his posting to Guantanamo. The base and all that it contained was U.S. property, an island in a hostile sea of red, surrounded by the enemy.

That rule had been in place since 1959, around the time Pyle's father was born, and there had never been an assault on the base.

Until now.

Three blasts, plastic explosives, and if Pyle had any lasting doubts, the sounds of automatic weapons fire confirmed what he already knew: this wasn't any exercise designed to test the camp's security procedures.

This was happening. The shit was coming down, and—

Pyle saw movement, fifty yards or so beyond the razor-wire perimeter he'd been assigned to guard. Raising his M-16, he sighted on the spot and saw a man rise from the undergrowth out there, with something balanced on his shoulder.

By the time Pyle recognized the object as a rocket launcher, triggering a short reflexive burst of 5.56 mm rounds in vain, the nose-heavy projectile was already hurtling toward him. All that he could do was hit the deck.

And pray.

Blue Ridge Mountains, Virginia

Mack Bolan listened as the all-news station playing on the Ford Explorer's radio kept coming back to it. Grim bulletins from Cuba, where a band of gunmen loosely dubbed insurgents had apparently stormed Camp X-Ray—the controversial, semisecret facility where U.S. Marines and CIA agents had penned alleged terrorist suspects since America's invasion of Afghanistan, in the wake of the 9/11 skyjacking raids. Civil libertarians called the military prison an illegal concentration camp and torture center, whose inmates were held without charges or counsel, some still publicly unnamed after all those years.

Administrators airily dismissed the charges, citing precedent from both world wars to justify their actions, and the controversy showed no signs of winding down while Camp X-Ray survived.

But now, it seemed, someone had tried another angle of attack to bring it down.

The early news was spotty, as expected. Getting any word out of Guantanamo was difficult enough, much less when the Marines and comrades from the Company were agitated by embarrassment. Bolan guessed that Hal Brognola would have the whole story—or most of it, at any rate—when he arrived at Stony Man Farm.

"YOU MADE GOOD TIME," Brognola said, shaking hands with Bolan on the farmhouse porch.

"It sounded urgent," Bolan said. "And I was in the neighborhood."

Almost, considering that Baltimore was more or less in Washington's backyard, both cities reasonably close to where the two men stood in summer sunshine, scanning cultivated fields to the north and west.

Brognola hadn't come to meet him on the porch alone. Beside the man from Justice stood the Farm's mission controller, Barbara Price. She had a private smile for Bolan, gripped his hand a heartbeat longer than was strictly necessary, then stepped back. No comment necessary.

"Bear's waiting for us in the War Room," Brognola said. "Do you want something to eat or drink, before we start? A chance to freshen up?"

"I'm fresh enough," Bolan replied. "Let's do it."

"Right."

They stepped inside the building and headed to the War Room, where Aaron Kurtzman, Stony Man's computer wizard, was waiting. A spinal gunshot, suffered in a raid that nearly doomed the Farm, had left him confined to a wheelchair for life, though it failed to snuff out his gregarious spirit. If Price was Stony Man's soul, then Kurtzman—"the Bear," to his friends—was its spark and its wry sense of humor.

Even so, he spared them any jokes that afternoon, greeting Bolan with a solemn face and a handshake strengthened by years of propelling himself on four wheels. Kurtzman shunned all the motorized scooters and chairs, determined to maintain the muscles that remained within his personal control.

Bolan sat at one end of a conference table that could seat a dozen comfortably, fifteen in a pinch. Brognola sat to his left, with Price directly opposite. Kurtzman assumed his place at the computer console, lowering a wide screen from its ceiling slot, at the table's far end.

"Is this about Guantanamo?" Bolan asked.

"Yes, and no," Brognola said. "It's too late for prevention, and that isn't our department, anyway. We'll leave that to the Corps and hope they get the bugs ironed out. No matter what, the raid's a fact of life—or history, by now, I guess you'd say."

"But it's not over," Bolan said.

"Unfortunately, no," Brognola answered, though it hadn't really been a question. "That's where we come in."

"Okay," the Executioner replied. "I'm listening. Why don't you give it to me from the top."

"What have you heard about Gitmo?" Brognola asked.

"The basics," Bolan replied. "Some kind of raid on Camp X-Ray, guerrillas by the sound of it. Some people are calling on the White House to invade and take Havana. No one seems to know if they were Cubans."

"I can answer that," Brognola said. "They weren't."

A nod to Kurtzman brought the first picture onto the screen. It was a mug shot, full face and profile, depicting a swarthy man with black hair and a mustache to match.

"We've had no luck getting the actual closed-circuit tapes," the big Fed explained, "but the Company claims it's identified both men in charge of the raiders. This is Sohrab Caspari, Iranian, a Shiite extremist linked to bombings and assassinations ranging from Baghdad to Singapore. He's thirty-six years old, a military veteran. You'll find the other details in his file."

"Ringleader?" Bolan asked.

"More like a partner," Brognola replied. "The raiders were divided into two distinct and separate teams."

Another nod produced a second face on-screen. This one was captured in a candid shot, a street scene somewhere in the Middle East, with shrouded women in the background, a street vendor off to one side. A hat shaded the man's face, and he was half-smiling to someone off camera, seemingly unaware of being caught on film.

"Asim Ben Muhunnad," Brognola said. "Age thirty-one, a Palestinian whose father, so I'm told, was in Fatah or Black September, maybe both at different times. So, Muhunnad got his fanaticism the old-fashioned way—he inherited it. Mossad's been tracking him since 1999. They've had a couple of near-misses, but he always slips away."

"Cuba's a long way from the Holy Land," Bolan observed.

"You'd think so, anyway," Brognola said. "Of course, we've seen the tendency of Muslim terrorists to strike world-wide against their enemies—in Europe, Indonesia, Africa, the States."

"Point taken. And Guantanamo was on the list because of the detainees?" Bolan asked.

"You're half right," Brognola agreed. "Except, this wasn't a punitive raid. It was a rescue mission," he explained. "A good, old-fashioned jailbreak."

"From Camp X-Ray?" Bolan said, sounding incredulous. "Inside a fortified Marine Corps base."

Brognola shrugged. "Sounds crazy, I'm the first one to admit. But who can argue with success? I mean, they pulled it off—up to a point, at least."

"The news I heard had nothing on a breakout," Bolan said. "Of course, it wouldn't, right?"

"They've kept that aspect under wraps, so far. How long the Corps and Washington can hold the lid in place is anybody's guess. Odds are, somebody in the Cuban press already knows the truth, or some of it, but anything they say or publish can be panned as Commie propaganda…for a while," Price said.

"Unless the runners surface publicly," Bolan suggested.

"Making statements," Brognola said. "Sending the media their videos. Or picking up where they left off, with new attacks."

"Sounds like a major PR problem," Bolan granted, "but the Cubans will most likely give them sanctuary under guard, the way they used to do with skyjackers."

"Maybe," Brognola said. "If they could find them."

"But…they haven't," Bolan said reluctantly.

"Not yet, according to our eyes there."

"Well, it's an island," Bolan said. "Where can they go?"

"With outside help," Brognola said, "the world's their oyster."

Bolan glowered at the screen, then asked, "Whose on the runner's list?"

"The raiders hit with thirty men, well-armed and well prepared with layouts for the base and Camp X-Ray," Brognola said. "They lost approximately two-thirds of their men, while taking out some thirty-five or forty U.S. personnel and wreaking havoc everywhere they went. That's part one of the hideous embarrassment.

"Part two is that the handful of survivors got away with nine inmates from Camp X-Ray. They probably went in hoping for more, but those they lifted are enough bad news to keep the Pentagon and White House sweating."

Kurtzman didn't need Brognola's nod this time. He keyed another picture, sending a third mug shot up on the screen. The latest subject had a thin, dark face, with jet-black curly hair and a prodigious, bristling uni-brow.

"I'll take them alphabetically," Brognola said. "This is Yasir Al Khalidha, Palestinian. Records say he's twenty-six years old, and a suspected member of al Qaeda. Emphasis on the suspected part, since he's resisted all interrogation methods used on him so far. The Company had no luck cracking him, and now they've lost their chance."

"Where was he captured?" Bolan asked.

"Afghanistan, 2002," Brognola answered. "He was fighting for the Taliban. No charges filed, so far—which, incidentally, is the case for all of those who made it out.

"All mug shots now, from X-Ray," Brognola added, as a fourth face filled the screen. This one was younger than its predecessors, but with a malicious cast.

"Farid Azima," Brognola announced. "Another Palestinian. Mossad connects him to Hamas. They want him for a dozen fatal bombings, all with multiple victims. We bagged him in Iraq, by chance."

"And didn't lock him up in Abu Ghraib?" Bolan asked.

"That's mostly for Iraqi nationals or tourists passing through. Despite his age—he just turned twenty-one—Azima is rated as a hard-case superstar. There was some talk of handing him to the Israelis, but I take it that the Company was interested in grilling him—for all the good it did them. Next."

An older face this time, bearded, showing a white scar at an angle through the left eyebrow. Another scar interrupted what was otherwise a flourishing mustache.

"Daywa Gul-Bashra," Brognola declared, by way of introduction. "From Afghanistan. At forty-four, he is the oldest of the fugitives, and also spent more time at X-Ray than the others. Special Forces nabbed him in the last week of December 2001. Tentative ID as an al Qaeda associate."

A forty-something face replaced Gul-Bashra's, glaring from the screen at those assembled in the War Room. Dark hair spilled across the pockmarked forehead, over narrow, angry eyes.

"Here's Emre Mandirali," Brognola said. "He's a Turkish national, age forty-two, arrested with a load of weapons in Afghanistan, nine months ago. As far as I can tell, he made it to Camp X-Ray based on his affiliation with the Turkish People's Liberation Army. Someone may have thought he'd spill the beans about an international connection. They were wrong. Next rabbit?"

Kurtzman put a seventh face on-screen. The first smile they had seen, so far, lit up a heart-shaped face framed by shoulder-length hair. A pointed goatee gave the smile a hint of mockery.

"Cirrus Mehrzad," Brognola said. "A twenty-nine-year-old Iranian, picked up in Baghdad eighteen months ago. Arresting officers found evidence that he was building IEDs—that's improvised explosive devices, Pentagon-speak for homemade bombs—and someone suggested he might be a link between Teheran and Iraqi insurgents."

"Seems cheerful enough," Bolan said.

"He's a talker, I'm told, but it comes down to nothing," Brognola replied. "Tries to ingratiate himself with his interrogators, blabbing up a storm about his family and what-not, but they come out on the other side of it with bupkus. Four to go."

On cue, another face took its place on-screen. Brognola gave his audience a moment to survey the deadpan countenance, marred by a crescent scar at the left corner of the mouth.

"Bahram Parwana," he declared, at last. "He and the next fellow you'll meet are both Afghanis, lifted from their homeland. This one got himself arrested in 2004, for sniping at a U.S. convoy."

"I'm surprised he made it," Bolan said.

"He nearly didn't," the big Fed acknowledged. "When our boys returned fire, this one took a shrapnel hit that knocked him out. The medics stitched him up and shipped him out. He's thirty-one, according to the records. Hasn't said a word to any of his jailers since they locked him up."

"The wound?" Bolan suggested.

"Nothing medical. He's just a stubborn son of a bitch," Brognola said. "Next slide."

The ninth fugitive looked younger than Bahram Parwana, if only by a year or two. His lean face was unmarked, except by worry lines around the eyes.

"Mahmood Tamwar," Hal said. "Age thirty, if you trust his file. Picked up in Kabul, in 2003, supposedly associated with al Qaeda and the Taliban. Also a heroin connection, which is nothing very special in Afghanistan, these days. Aaron?"

The next face had a youthful look, despite the salt-and-pepper beard. Wire-rimmed glasses with a cracked left lens magnified hazel eyes under glowering brows. The mouth was a bloodless slash beneath a meaty nose.

"Ishaq Uthman," Hal said. "Egyptian, thirty-six years old, ex-military and associated with a remnant of the gang that killed Sadat. What he was doing in Iraq is anybody's guess. Lord knows he hasn't dropped a hint to any of the X-Ray experts."

"No al Qaeda ties?" Bolan asked.

"Nothing on the record," Brognola replied. "For what that's worth. Last one."

The final face was solemn but serene, the scalp clean-shaved over thin brows, with a close-trimmed beard. The upper lip was scarred by childhood surgery to correct a cleft palate.

"Last but not least, we have Ghulam Yazid," Brognola declared. "He's a thirty-year-old Pakistani, busted in Afghanistan last year, after a border crossing. Guns and ammunition were recovered, plus a message from Osama's minions to the Taliban. That bought Yazid a ticket overseas, but he has not been, shall we say, forthcoming during his interrogations."

"There's a shocker," Price remarked.

"Indeed. And that's the lot. Long story short, we need to round them up or bury them before they mount new operations on their own, or as a group."

"But no one knows exactly where they are," Bolan said, stating it as fact and not a question.

"Hey," Brognola answered him, "if it was easy, we'd all be retired."

"Terrific," Bolan said. "Where should I start?"

THE DOSSIER CONTAINED sparse information on the fugitives, a bit more on their liberators and two pages on the contact who'd be waiting for the Executioner when he got to Cuba. The short bio told him that Maria Santos was a thirty-three-year-old contract employee of the CIA, whose day job as a tourist guide allowed her contact with outsiders visiting Cuba.

Her photographs showed Bolan that Santos was a Latina looker, with long dark hair, surprising blue eyes and a body reminiscent of Raquel Welch in her prime.

Bolan would travel as Matt Cooper of Toronto, on a Canadian passport. Stony Man's forgeries were impeccable, and he had no worries about clearing Customs. The hassle would come afterward, when he and Santos began seeking their quarry on an island with over eleven million residents.

That was, assuming the nine fugitives and their surviving liberators were still on the island. If not, as Brognola had stated, the world was their oyster.

And none of them would be afraid to crack it open, given half a chance.

2

Straits of Florida

"Full speed ahead," Captain Arnold Bateman said, peering through his binoculars at open sea before the *Tropic Princess*. From the giant cruise ship's bridge, he had the vantage of a man standing atop a twelve-story hotel, with no clouds overhead and nothing to obstruct his view to eastward.

In fact, the *Tropic Princess* looked like a hotel that had been set adrift somehow, as if by magic, floating on the sea when it should logically be squatting on a corner of Park Avenue or the Las Vegas Strip. The ship measured 960 feet from bow to stern and weighed 115,000 tons. Beneath the captain's feet, three thousand passengers were anxiously awaiting the vacation of a lifetime, while twelve hundred crew members and entertainers worked around the clock to meet the needs of paying customers—and to keep the behemoth afloat.

During a classic two-week cruise, the British captain's passengers were treated to a taste of Cuba, the Bahamas, the Dominican Republic, Puerto Rico, Trinidad-Tobago, Venezuela and Jamaica. Shore excursions granted them the opportunity to browse and carouse in each port.

It was not all island-hopping, though. For those who truly loved to cruise, the ship was self-contained, permitting them to pass the full two weeks in luxury without ever setting foot on dry land. The ship featured seven restaurants, three swimming pools and seven spas, a dinner theater and cabaret, a discotheque, a first-run cinema, three gymnasiums, a fully staffed infirmary and a casino.

Most days, the captain liked his job. Granted, some passengers were no better than spoiled children, posing as adults, but Bateman managed to avoid them for the most part, choosing only a select few for the honored nightly ritual of dining at the captain's table. Minors were excluded, and his steward had an eye for younger women, well endowed, whose husbands or companions didn't mind the captain peering at their cleavage over cocktails and filet mignon.

On balance, Bateman worried more about his crew than any of his passengers. Despite the smiling photos the cruise line printed in its various brochures, some of the employees were a surly lot, uneducated, and the screening process left a lot to be desired. Substance abuse and petty theft were more or less routine. Some members of the crew engaged in smuggling; others moonlighted as prostitutes or gigolos.

So far, the present cruise had been smooth sailing, both in terms of weather and the human element. There'd been no quarrels among the passengers or crew, no incidents ashore demanding Bateman's intervention. If his luck held, they could all relax and—

Bateman lowered his binoculars and turned, facing two new arrivals on the bridge. He sometimes welcomed passengers topside, by invitation only, but the swarthy men who stood before him now were strangers, neither members of his crew nor anyone whom Bateman would've chosen to observe the inner workings of the ship.

Wearing a corporate smile, he asked, "How may I help you, gentlemen?"

The guns seemed to appear from nowhere, one of them pointed at Bateman's face.

"If you cooperate with us," its owner said, "perhaps no one aboard this ship will die today."

SOHRAB CASPARI THOUGHT, *It almost seems too easy*. After all the planning, all the risk, the bloody skirmish at Guantanamo, the capture of the *Tropic Princess* struck him almost as an anticlimax, disappointing in its stark simplicity.

But it was done.

Beside him, Osman Zarghona, his Afghani second in command, covered the bridge crew with his AKSU assault rifle, while Caspari kept his Uzi submachine gun leveled at the gray-haired captain. In addition to their main automatic weapons, both hijackers also carried pistols, hand grenades and knives.

"Is this some kind of joke?" the captain asked.

"Perhaps I should kill one of your men, to see if we are joking. Yes?" Caspari answered.

"No. That won't be necessary," the captain said. "What, exactly, do you want?"

"Before we speak of that," Caspari said, "know that we aren't alone. I have more men aboard your ship, with weapons and enough explosives to destroy it."

"I see." The captain frowned and said, "How many gun-men—"

"Freedom fighters!" Zarghona snapped.

"Yes, of course. How many *freedom fighters* are there, may I ask?"

"Enough to do the job," Caspari told him. Fishing in his left-hand pocket for a cell phone, he explained, "I keep in touch through this. The marvels of technology. You only see them—hear them—if and when I say. Follow instructions, and your passengers may suffer no disturbance."

"As to these instructions," Captain Bateman said, "what might they be?"

"We have demands," Caspari answered, "which you will broadcast over your radio. Freedom for comrades wrongfully imprisoned. Reparation payments. Other things. If the Americans defy us, then we will be forced to execute your passengers and crew."

"Don't take offense, old chap," the captain said, "but you've been misinformed. This ship is not American. Its owners are Italians, Greeks—one Saudi, I believe. It's registered in Panama. I doubt that Washington will care what happens to the *Tropic Princess.* Certainly, they won't negotiate with…freedom fighters, like yourselves."

"You think me foolish, yes?" Caspari said, sneering. "That is a serious mistake. We know that half your passengers are from the U.S.A. They cannot visit Cuba from America, so rich pigs fly to Mexico and board your ship. All this is public knowledge. Glory to the Internet."

"I grant you that we have Americans aboard," Bateman replied. "I'm simply saying that—"

"You say too much!" Caspari snapped. "Is time for you to listen, now. You *will* broadcast our very fair and just demands, or face the consequences of defiance. Must I demonstrate by executing someone here and now? That one, perhaps?"

Caspari swung his Uzi toward a young man standing frozen, several paces to the captain's left. The target blanched and trembled in his crisp white uniform.

"No, please!" the captain blurted. "I'm simply trying to prepare you for the disappointment you will face in bargaining with the Americans."

"I fear no disappointment," Caspari said. "I and all my men are quite prepared to die. Your passengers and crew, I think, value their lives and comfort more than principle."

The captain's shoulders slumped. "You have a list, for my communications officer?"

"His services are not required," Caspari said. "Prepare the radio and stand aside, while I address the world."

"Of course," Bateman said. "As you wish. About your other men…"

Caspari checked his wristwatch. "I must speak to them in nineteen minutes, and at each half hour after that." He nodded toward Zarghona and explained, "Should either of us fail to make contact on schedule, it means the destruction of your ship."

"I understand," Bateman replied. "We pose no threat to you. Which one of you will follow me to the communications room?"

Washington, D.C.

NABI ULMALHAMA HELD A wooden match precisely one inch below the square-cut tip of his Cuban cigar. He spent a moment savoring the taste of rum-soaked tobacco leaves, then reached out for his glass of twenty-year-old scotch.

Strict Muslim teachings barred the use of alcoholic beverages, but Ulmalhama reckoned that God granted dispensation for selected, special servants of His cause.

Listening to early-evening traffic rumble past his posh Georgetown apartment, Ulmalhama nearly missed the deferential knocking on his study door.

"Enter," he said.

His houseman crossed the thick carpet silently, half-bowed to Ulmalhama as he said, "Sir, if you care to watch the news?"

"Of course."

Waiting until the houseman left him, Ulmalhama picked up the remote control and switched on his giant flat-screen television, flicking through the channels until he found CNN. A blond reporter stood before a cruise ship, speaking urgently into a handheld microphone. The dateline banner covering her breasts told Ulmalhama she was in Miami. He pressed another button to increase the volume.

"The ship is much like the one behind me, only somewhat larger. Now, we understand the *Tropic Princess* is the flagship of the Argos Cruise Line, launched in June 2006. It can accommodate three thousand passengers. And I'm told the ship is booked to full capacity this evening, after taking on new passengers in Cuba. With the crew, we make it four thousand two hundred people presently aboard the *Tropic Princess,* hijacked in the Straits of Florida."

The station cut away to a grim-looking anchorman. The newsman said, "We now have audio from the hijackers on the Argos cruise ship, broadcasting a list of their demands over an open frequency. This signal was recorded ten minutes ago, from the *Tropic Princess* in international waters. We air it now, for the first time."

Ulmalhama sat and listened, with his eyes closed, to the gruff, familiar voice.

"I am Sohrab Caspari. Yesterday, with comrades from Allah's Warriors, I was privileged to liberate a number of political prisoners from the American death camp at Cuba's Guantanamo Bay. Some of those hostages are now with me, aboard the *Tropic Princess,* a decadent pleasure craft symbolizing all that is wrong with corrupt Western society. We have more than four thousand prisoners on board, whom we will gladly execute unless the following demands are met.

"First, we demand the immediate liberation of all remaining prisoners held at Guantanamo Bay, at Abu Ghraib prison in Baghdad, and throughout the state of Israel. A list of names shall be provided to the White House, but since many of the prisoners are held illegally and incommunicado, we can only estimate their total number. To avoid useless debate, after the prisoners identified by name are freed, we expect the liberation of one martyr for each man, woman and child aboard the *Tropic Princess*."

Ulmalhama smiled at that. It was a nice touch, which would get them nowhere.

As intended.

"Second, we demand a ransom of one million dollars for each hostage presently aboard the ship. To spare ourselves the effort of precisely counting them, we shall accept four billion dollars as the total ransom. Payments of one billion dollars each shall be wired to four separate bank accounts, one each in Switzerland, Liechtenstein, the Cayman Islands and in Costa Rica. Relevant transfer information shall be provided upon acceptance of our terms by Washington."

Another hopeless cause, Ulmalhama thought. It was perfect.

"Finally, we want a helicopter capable of seating fourteen passengers, in addition to the crew. This aircraft shall be used for our evacuation of the *Tropic Princess,* with one hostage for each member of my team. The helicopter shall be capable of traveling five hundred miles without refueling.

"If the President of the United States does not agree to meet our terms within four hours of the present time—that is, by 9:00 p.m.—we shall begin to execute the hostages in groups of ten, at thirty-minute intervals. Execution of the final hostages shall thus occur eight days and eighteen hours from the present time. Any attempt at rescue shall, of course, result in the immediate destruction of the ship and all on board. Good day."

Nabi Ulmalhama switched off his TV set before the long-faced anchor could express his shock and outrage. So far, phase two of his plan was proceeding on schedule.

Well satisfied, the Saudi rose and poured another glass of whiskey to accompany his fine cigar.

MACK BOLAN HAD ALMOST finished packing when the news came over CNN. He'd sat with Barbara Price and Aaron Kurtzman, listening to the recorded voice of terror, emanating from a man he'd just been asked to track down and eliminate.

Fourteen seats aboard the exit chopper, with one hostage for each hijacker, told Bolan that a seven-man crew had seized the *Tropic Princess.* Their small number was the good news *and* the bad.

Six targets made the hunting relatively simple, until Bolan realized that they would be dispersed among four thousand innocents, no doubt prepared to kill at random in the face of any challenge. Furthermore, he had to think about Sohrab Caspari's final threat, *immediate destruction of the ship and all on board,* in the event of an attempted rescue.

"How much C-4 would they need to sink a ship that size?" he asked Kurtzman. "And how long would it take?"

"I'll crunch some numbers."

Brognola's call came through, and Price put it on the speakerphone. "We're all here, Hal," she said.

"Okay. You've heard the news, about the *Tropic Princess?*"

"Watching it right now," Price said.

"You won't be shocked to hear the Man is standing firm. We don't negotiate with terrorists, full stop. In fact, we couldn't meet their terms in any case. Suppose we cut loose everyone at Camp X-Ray and Abu Ghraib, gave them the cash and chopper. The Israelis still won't budge on prisoners. The hijackers had to know that, going in."

"So, what's the play?" Bolan asked.

"Change of plans," Brognola said. "You won't be flying into Cuba after all. We're putting you on board a submarine. We'll chopper you to Norfolk Naval Base and let the swabbies carry on from there. Take anything you think you might need, as long as you can carry it and pass the odd police inspection."

"Well, that trims my shopping list," Bolan replied.

"Your contact should be current on the local hardware outlets," Brognola said.

"And where's the rendezvous?" Bolan asked.

"Ask the Navy," Brognola replied. "Somewhere mid-Atlantic, I expect. Questions?"

"None from me," Bolan responded.

"Great. I'll try to keep you updated en route. After you go ashore, we've got the sat phones, but use them sparingly. Try not to tangle with the Cuban army or security police, but if you have to, don't let them take you."

"Or you'll disavow all knowledge," Bolan finished for him. "Got it." He broke the link to Washington.

"A submarine?" Price said. "Instead of flying?"

"It's a rush job," Bolan said. "The other way, I have to fly to Mexico, then wait for a connecting flight into Havana. This ought to cut the time by half, at least."

"For just a second there, I thought he wanted them to help you board the *Tropic Princess*."

Bolan frowned and shook his head. "Too late for that. They'd see me coming, and I'd never get the shooters sorted out among four thousand passengers and crew before they did their worst."

"Who do you think will handle it?" Kurtzman asked.

Bolan shrugged, already on his feet and moving toward the exit. "Navy SEALs or Delta Force could try it, but you've got a Panamanian ship in international waters."

"I'll get the chopper ready," Price said. "Need any help collecting gear?"

"I'm good," Bolan said. "See you on the deck in fifteen, tops."

EMRE MANDIRALI UNDERSTOOD his mission, but he found it difficult to keep a low profile, moving among his fellow passengers as if he was another drone on holiday, smiling and nodding foolishly at strangers, when he longed to let them see the mini-Uzi he carried in his gym bag, or the pistol tucked beneath his baggy, floral-patterned shirt.

To let them *hear* his weapons, better yet.

How sweet it would have been to rake the decks with automatic fire, watching his targets twitch and fall. Or tossing hand grenades into the restaurants where they lined up to gorge themselves like pigs at the trough.

But Mandirali had his orders, and despite his grueling months in prison, his abiding rage against those who'd caged him, he had discipline enough to do as he was told in combat situations. He could wait, knowing that it would soon be time to kill.

Barring disaster, Mandirali knew his leader, who had liberated him from vile captivity, had to now control the *Tropic Princess*. He would issue the demands they had agreed upon, and Washington would solemnly announce its policy against rewarding terrorists. Sohrab Caspari's deadline would elapse, and then the killing could begin in earnest.

Mandirali harbored no illusions where his future was concerned. While in prison, he had prayed to Allah for a chance to strike out once more at his enemies and be avenged, before he claimed his place in Paradise.

He knew there would be no release of prisoners, no ransom payment, certainly no helicopter sent to carry them away. While Mandirali couldn't guess precisely how he'd die, he guessed that members of some military hostage-rescue team would storm the ship, sparking a chain reaction of events that would be seen as tragic in the Western world, while warriors of the one true faith proclaimed another stunning victory.

With any luck, he thought, the final body count might well exceed the famous 9/11 raids.

Mandirali himself would achieve no such triumph, but he was a part of the team. By now, his comrades should have C-4 charges planted at strategic points below the waterline, where they would detonate in sequence, gut the *Princess* when her would-be saviors came aboard.

Ideally the event would be broadcast on live television.

As soon as any would-be rescuers appeared, his orders were to fire at will, inflict as many casualties as he could manage in his brief remaining time on Earth.

The plastic explosives would do the worst damage, trapping hundreds belowdecks as seawater flooded the vessel, starting fires that would ignite the ship's fuel stores, turning the whole vast hulk into a sunken tomb and smorgasbord for scavengers.

It was enough to make him smile in earnest as he passed among the sheep, nodding in mock friendship and wishing they were already in hell.

3

Under other circumstances, Bolan might have appreciated the scenery passing below the Bell JctRanger, but part of his mind was on board the *Tropic Princess* with her passengers and crew, the rest trying to work out where the other team of terrorists would strike.

Nine prisoners had broken out of Camp X-Ray, with an estimated six surviving raiders. Sohrab Caspari, speaking for the *Tropic Princess* hijackers, had demanded a chopper with seating for seven gunmen and an equal number of human shields. That left eight targets unaccounted for.

Where would they surface?

Were they still in Cuba? And if so, what worthwhile targets were available?

Brognola would be puzzling over that in Washington, together with the Pentagon, the CIA, the State Department—anyone, in fact, who could provide a hint of insight on the problem and anticipate the next move by their enemies.

He was too late to help the *Tropic Princess,* and it preyed on Bolan's mind, but maybe he would be in time to stop the other team from acting out whatever bloody drama that its leaders planned.

The bad news was that Caspari's team had already escaped from Cuba. If Asim Ben Muhunnad's strike team had also fled the island, they might turn up anywhere. Each passing hour gave them greater range.

And if they surfaced somewhere outside Cuba, Bolan's visit to the island would be a colossal waste of time. He would be sidelined once again, waiting for transport to the battle zone or relegated to a spectator's position, while the action went ahead without him.

Eyes sweeping the horizon, he resigned himself to wait and see what happened next. He couldn't force the confrontation, couldn't read his adversary's mind and force Muhunnad into some act ahead of schedule.

Bolan preferred proactive strategy, whenever possible, but in the present situation he could only bide his time, reacting to the moves made by his enemies. The best that he could do, in terms of preparation, was to stand in readiness and hope Muhunnad's fugitive guerrillas chose a target close enough for Bolan to respond in a timely fashion, without placing any innocents in needless jeopardy.

"Another twenty minutes, sir," his pilot said.

Bolan responded with a nod and focused on the journey still ahead.

Cuba

ASIM BEN MUHUNNAD WAS NOT accustomed to a life of luxury. But nothing in his wildest dreams had prepared him for Bahia Matanzas.

The five-star resort was located on the island's northwest coast, an oasis of luxury in a country known for its rural poverty and urban decay.

The resort was a landmark on the road to restoration of Cuba's crippled tourist industry. It offered Canadians, Britons and others a taste of tropic luxury not seen in Cuba since

Batista's time. The posh resort possessed a golf course and all the other amenities required to steal jet-setters from Aruba, Nassau, Martinique, Barbados, Montserrat, or Guadalupe.

The facility was close to full capacity. Its owners didn't know that eight of the vacationers in residence were using stolen cash and credit cards, but meant to pay their final tab in blood.

Bahia Matanzas.

It pleased Muhunnad that the name, translated from Spanish to English, meant Massacre Bay.

CASPARI LITERALLY SAW the CH-60 Seahawk helicopter coming from a mile away. It showed up first on radar, gaining on the *Tropic Princess* from the northwest, presumably from a naval base in Florida. Caspari knew the aircraft had to be filled with television news reporters or a strike force of commandos sent to kill him.

When he saw its U.S. Navy markings with his own eyes, all doubt vanished.

By that time, he had issued orders via cell phone to his soldiers circulating through the ship. Farid Azima had not answered, a disturbing problem Caspari could not deal with at the moment, but the rest were at their stations, standing by to act upon his order.

When the Navy helicopter made its first pass overhead, Caspari had six passengers already standing on the cruise ship's Sun Deck, situated below and in front of the bridge with its broad tinted windows. Daywa Gul-Bashra had collected them with offers of special tour, then showed his weapon to them when they reached the open deck. They were lined up near the railing, hands clasped atop their heads, some of them weeping as they faced the open sea nine stories down, Gul-Bashra just behind them with his submachine gun leveled at their backs.

Two women and four men. Caspari didn't know them,

didn't care who any of them were or where they came from. They'd been picked at random, as examples for the infidels who had defied him.

"Reach out to the helicopter with your radio," Caspari ordered. "Make contact at once."

It took a moment, but a man's voice issued from the speakers mounted around the bridge. "We hear you, people. Captain Ernest Ryan, here. Who am I talking to?"

"The man in charge," Caspari answered. "Since you've been sent to intercept us, I assume that you're aware of our demands."

"I read the list," Ryan replied.

"And you are now in violation of the ultimatum. Naturally there are penalties for your arrogance."

"Hold on, now!" Ryan shouted.

"Can you see the people on the Sun Deck?"

"Yeah," Ryan said. "I see them."

"Watch and learn."

Caspari keyed the cell phone, just a single ring, the arranged signal. Fifty feet beyond the bridge and twenty feet below it, Gul-Bashra sprayed his six targets with automatic fire, stitching them from left to right and back again before they fell. Four collapsed onto the deck, while two others pitched over the rail and fell toward the ocean far below.

Gul-Bashra wasted no time scuttling back to cover, while the helicopter hovered, angry faces pressed against its windows.

Captain Ryan raged, "Goddamn you, listen—"

"No! *You* listen," Caspari snapped. "Six passengers are dead because you came here to attack us. Sixty more will die at once, if you attempt to board the ship. If one of you survives to set foot on the deck, I will sink the *Tropic Princess*. Are we clear?"

There was silence from the circling helicopter.

"*Are we clear?*" Caspari bellowed.

"We're clear," Ryan replied. "We're backing off now."

"Any tricks," Caspari said, "and four thousand deaths are on your head."

Washington, D.C.

"PERFECT," NABI ULMALHAMA whispered to the empty room. The events unfolding on the television screen pleased him no end.

The only disappointment, so far, was a simple case of network censorship. Apparently there'd been at least one camera aboard the helicopter that had carried men and guns to liberate the *Tropic Princess*. It had captured the events on deck, and the resultant tape had found its way to CNN headquarters, but the editors in charge of on-air content had deleted footage of the sacrificial lambs as bullets ripped into their twitching bodies and the fell.

Never mind, Ulmalhama thought. In a few more hours, it would all be on the Internet for everyone to see worldwide.

Now that the first knee-jerk reflex had passed, now that the Pentagon had flexed its muscles and discovered it was powerless, he could begin to watch the clock again.

Two hours and fifteen minutes were left until the next round of bloodletting should begin. It would be dark over the ocean, or nearly so, but cruise ships were like giant office buildings, lighted day and night. He wondered whether any more helicopters would approach the *Tropic Princess* as the deadline neared.

He hoped so, hoped it would be broadcast live this time, with nothing spared. It would be educational for enemies of Allah to behold His work firsthand.

The telephone purred at his elbow. Ulmalhama muted the TV and lifted the receiver midway through its second ring.

At once, he recognized the voice of his immediate superior at the Saudi consulate.

"Of course, sir," Ulmalhama said. "I'm watching the reports now, as we speak… It's terrible, I certainly agree… Sohrab Caspari? No, sir. He's Iranian, my sources guarantee it…. Yes, by all means, he should tell the President that we are not involved in any way."

His smile returned as he replaced the telephone receiver in its cradle. Even now, Saudi Arabia's ambassador would have his telephone in hand, prepared to call the White House and insist, with all due deference, that no official of the Saudi government had any knowledge of the raid against Guantanamo or the hijacking of the *Tropic Princess*.

It was almost true.

Except for Ulmalhama, no one in Riyadh or any of the desert nation's scattered consulates was privy to the plan.

Norfolk, Virginia

BOLAN WAS BARELY OFF the chopper, ducking underneath the swirl of rotor blades, when a lieutenant dressed in navy blue approached, holding his cap in place with one hand, and declared, "I've got bad news."

"Let's hear it," Bolan said.

The story was a short one, quickly told. A squad of SEALs had planned to board the *Tropic Princess,* and the terrorists had executed half a dozen hostages. Now, with the deadline drawing closer, everyone was bracing for a bloodbath.

"We've got your transportation standing by," the man said.

His second chopper of the evening was a big Sikorsky SH-3 Sea King, complete with two-man crew and seating for a maximum of thirty passengers. Bolan strapped in close to the cockpit, slipped on his earphones and wedged his single bag between his feet.

Liftoff pressed Bolan back into his seat. He had his second airborne view of the Norfolk Naval Complex within fifteen minutes, as the Sea King rose and circled, found its heading and proceeded out to sea.

The grim news from the *Tropic Princess* left him all the more determined to do everything within his power to corral the second band of terrorists at large and stop whatever mad scheme they were planning to pursue.

He knew the pilots would inform him when they found the submarine and made arrangements for the transfer. In the meantime, Bolan wasn't flying tourist class. He was a warrior bound for battle with an enemy who could be anywhere, preparing to do anything.

And all he could do was wait.

4

Cuba

"Is everyone in place?" Asim Ben Muhunnad inquired.

"Yes, sir," said his second in command, Sarsour Ibn Tabari. "I positioned them myself, with strict instructions."

"Cell phones on?"

"Of course."

"We're ready, then."

"Ready," his number two agreed.

Muhunnad carried a map of the resort folded in his pocket, but he had already memorized the winding paths, the layout of the various beach cottages and hotel towers, swimming pools and spas. He could find his way around the resort blindfolded. He knew where each one of his six gunmen should be right now, as they prepared to seize control.

And anyone who failed him was a dead man.

Muhunnad and his warriors had concealed their weapons and explosives in their luggage, on arrival at Bahia Matanzas, but the Cuban climate made it impractical for them to wear trench coats or other garments convenient for hiding military hardware. He had suggested beach robes and towels or blankets, soft-drink coolers, baggy shirts and trousers, shopping bags from any of the several boutiques and shops at the resort.

Once their intentions were revealed, discretion wouldn't matter anymore.

Muhunnad himself had picked a more sophisticated get-up for himself and for Tabari. Over the past half hour, they had lured two resort employees to their bungalow, forcing both men to shed their uniforms at gunpoint, then killed both and left them in the bathtub.

Muhunnad and Tabari, dressed in the stolen uniforms—white peasant shirts, with matching shorts—walked side-by-side along one of the concrete paths that made the beach resort a kind of maze, while guaranteeing privacy for guests who spent big money on the beachfront cottages. Tabari pushed a large housekeeping cart, their folding-stock Kalashnikov assault rifles concealed inside a drooping sack filled to the brim with crumpled sheets. Grenades rested beneath an old towel, in the mop bucket. Pistols were warm against their belly skin, under the baggy shirts.

Thus rendered more or less invisible to paying guests, as well as other personnel at the resort, Muhunnad and Tabari skirted swimming pools where women bared their bodies in obscene bikinis, slurping alcohol and teasing men who lusted after them. They passed an outdoor restaurant, where fat white people gorged themselves on delicacies common folk could not afford. At last, they found the service entrance to the main hotel block, used a key card taken from one of the men they'd killed and passed inside.

The plan became a trifle dicey after that, since ordinary personnel were rarely admitted to the executive offices at Bahia Matanzas. Those who made that walk were generally bound for termination, over some offense against the rules prescribed by management.

Muhunnad and Tabari were about to break that rule.

They took the service elevator down one level, to the basement office block. Still trundling the cleaning cart, they moved along a spotless corridor until they reached the door they sought.

Muhunnad turned the doorknob, shoved the door open and held it while Tabari pushed his cart inside. A pretty secretary paused in the act of shutting down her personal computer for the day and frowned at them.

"What's this?" she asked. "You're not supposed to be here yet."

Muhunnad and Tabari whipped their automatic rifles from the linen bag and aimed them at the woman. "If you make a sound, you die," Muhunnad said.

She made a little squeak, but the Palestinian forgave her, in consideration of the circumstances.

"Now," Muhunnad said. "We wish to speak with your employer, Mr. Quentin Avery."

She led them past her desk, down a short hallway, to the manager's office. It had not surprised Muhunnad in the least to learn that the man in overall charge of Bahia Matanzas was a white Canadian.

What else could one expect, these days?

The secretary rapped on Avery's door, then opened it without waiting for his summons. Muhunnad and Tabari entered, one rifle covering each of their two hostages.

Avery, a pink-faced, balding man, gaped at the strangers and their guns, then found his voice. "What's the meaning of this?" he demanded.

"It means," Muhunnad answered, "that your property is now under new management. If you agree to our demands, you may survive."

Canal de Yucatán

"TEN MINUTES, SIR," the Sea King's pilot said, "before we rendezvous with the *Poseidon*."

"Copy," Bolan answered, just to let the flyboy know that he was still awake.

The officers and crew of the *Poseidon* had to put Bolan ashore on Cuba without tipping off local authorities to his arrival. As to how or when he'd leave the island, if and when it came to that, details were still up in the air.

The copilot came back to deal with Bolan's transfer to the submarine. The gear he carried resembled a parachute harness, minus the pack and chute. Bolan stood and slipped it on, cinched up its several buckles, then stood easy while the copilot made sure he'd done the job correctly.

"Quick releases here, here and here," the flyboy said, tapping each safety catch in turn. "Don't use them, though, unless you wind up in the water. Shouldn't happen, but it does, sometimes."

"Noted," Bolan replied.

"Another strap here, for your bag," the copilot said. "Leaves your hands free for the cable."

Bolan double-strapped the smallish bag to his left hip, then accepted gloves and goggles from the navy airman. Putting on the goggles meant removing his headphones. The copilot replaced them with a set of earmuffs lacking any common link.

"Expect some spray," the airman told him, now required to shout. "It's unavoidable. They'll have dry clothes for you on board."

"I hear you."

"Ready?"

Bolan nodded.

"Right. Stand in the door."

A sea monster had risen underneath them while they hovered in the air, discussing spray and buckles. It was more than five hundred feet long, with water still sluicing from its flanks and conning tower, swirls of foam still visible on deck.

As Bolan stood and watched, a hatch opened some thirty feet in front of the *Poseidon*'s conning tower.

Bolan felt the light tap on his shoulder, used both hands to grip the cable fastened to his harness overhead and stepped out into space. The chopper lowered him serenely, like a hand-cranked bucket going down into a well.

The salt spray started whipping at him when he was approximately halfway down. The helicopter's downdraft set him slowly spinning, but it didn't spoil his view of sailors scrambling through the open hatch below, to stand on the *Poseidon*'s forward deck. Bolan supposed that two of them were there to help him from his harness and get him below-decks, while the third was sent to supervise.

It was the military way.

He touched down on the deck without a spill into the sea, and seconds later Bolan was without his rigging, saw it hoisting back into the air. An ensign welcomed him aboard without much warmth and led the way below, Bolan's two escorts steering and supporting him until he found his sea legs.

Poseidon's skipper met him with a handshake, introduced himself as Captain Walter Gossage, and led Bolan to the conning tower, aft. Some of the seamen watched them pass, but most attended to their duties and ignored the Executioner.

"I don't know what you heard while you were airborne," Gossage said, when they were standing underneath the conning tower, "but I've got bad news."

"I'm getting used to it," Bolan replied.

"Okay. Seems that the people you've been looking for have taken over a resort in Cuba. Bahia Matanzas. Ever heard of it?"

The warrior shook his head.

"I hadn't either," Gossage told him, "but I've got coordinates. We're on our way."

Washington, D.C.

BROGNOLA HAD BEEN WAITING for the call. He answered on the first ring of his secure line and recognized Mack Bolan's voice at once.

"How many hostages?" Bolan asked.

"Based on what we have from corporate headquarters, in Toronto, there should be about eleven hundred. Two or three hundred employees, all depending on the day and time."

"I'll see what I can do," Bolan said.

"Stay in touch, if possible."

"Will do."

The line went dead without a sign-off, something Brognola had gotten used to over time. Bolan was information-oriented, sometimes short on the amenities, which suited him just fine.

They had a bloody job of work to do, and pleasantries were strictly out of place.

He thought about the murdered hostages aboard the *Tropic Princess.* He had seen the uncut tape, shot by a member of the SEAL team, and while he had seen much worse over the course of his career, the casual brutality still left him angry and unsettled.

Brognola tried to follow Bolan in his mind, tracked the *Poseidon* on its run to Bahia Matanzas, where he would meet his contact on the island.

Brognola knew nothing of Maria Santos, beyond what he'd read in her slim CIA dossier. He hoped she wouldn't clash with Bolan, wouldn't slow him too much or screw things up somehow by getting squeamish in the crunch. If she knew what was coming, understood how much it meant to all concerned, maybe she'd be all right.

Maybe—and maybe not.

Cuba

MARIA SANTOS LIT a cigarette, cursing her lack of will-power even as she inhaled and felt the first sweet kick of nicotine. She had quit smoking two weeks earlier, but now resumed the habit almost without conscious thought, while waiting in the darkness for a stranger who could change—or end—her life.

That life was tense enough without the latest complication. In fact, Santos led two lives: one as a dutiful and conscientious secretary for the Cuban Ministry of Agriculture in Havana, and another as a contract agent for the CIA. One was an exercise in tedium that paid her bills; the other added spice—and danger—to an otherwise mundane existence bounded by her daytime job, a small circle of uninspiring friends, and dates with men who came expecting sex as payback for a cheap meal in a dreary restaurant.

She could have chosen to decline the job—she had considered it, in fact; but she finally agreed, feeling a sense of obligation that confused her even now. She'd been relieved when half of the escapees turned up on the *Tropic Princess,* sailing off into the sunset with their mostly Anglo hostages, taking the problem far away from her.

Now, this.

The terrorists at Bahia Matanzas couldn't sail away. They couldn't fly—or, rather, most of them could not—because the resort's helicopter seated only four passengers, in addition to the pilot. They couldn't even drive or *walk* away, now that the Cuban army and security police had thrown a ring of men and guns around the great resort's eight hundred acres.

They were trapped, in fact, together with their hostages.

So, how, in God's name, did the CIA expect her to transport a stranger—an American—past all the watchers, snipers and patrols, to penetrate Bahia Matanzas? The thought had distressed her, at first.

And then she had an idea.

Santos only hoped the stranger who was on his way to meet her, Matt Cooper, was able to perform the trick she had in mind.

The plan she had devised for Bahia Matanzas put her life at risk, not just her job and liberty. If caught, she might be executed on the spot, without even the semblance of a trial. But if she didn't try, Santos knew that she would always feel as if the blood of murdered hostages was on her hands.

That was ridiculous, she realized, but logic held no sway over emotion.

Stubbing out her cigarette, she reached for another, then drew back her hand. She would make herself wait a while longer. Ten minutes, or maybe fifteen. An exercise in discipline, to occupy her mind while she waited for the stranger from America.

The man who, if he wasn't skilled and very careful, just might get her killed.

THE EXECUTIONER double-checked the minimal gear that he'd brought with him from the Farm. He had his shoulder rig for the Beretta 93-R, two spare magazines—making it sixty rounds, in all—and a commando dagger honed to razor-sharpness, in a lightweight nylon sheath.

That hardware wouldn't see him through what lay ahead, but Bolan had to wait and see what was available once he arrived in Cuba and made contact with Maria Santos. Given Cuban history over the past half century, Bolan expected Russian weapons to predominate, along with knockoffs from the former Eastern Bloc and certain lethal toys produced in South America. In terms of weaponry, Bolan could handle anything that came his way. He only hoped that it would be reliable and accurate, with ammunition plentiful enough to see him through the bloody work ahead.

And he had no illusions as to what was waiting for him, if and when he made his way inside Bahia Matanzas. The eight hostage takers were desperate men, religious fanatics with nothing to lose but their lives—and those lives, Bolan guessed, were already written off as lost in their own minds. The whole bizarre event, from Gitmo to the latest series of impossible demands, smelled like a kamikaze mission from the start.

That understanding altered Bolan's mission from a hostage rescue to search-and-destroy. Taking for granted that the terrorists were bent on killing their roughly twelve hundred prisoners, once they had managed to insult America as much as possible on international TV, he had to find a way inside and neutralize the enemy before they carried out their plan.

For some at Bahia Matanzas, Bolan guessed, he might already be too late. They had a deadline coming up, and Bolan might not be there to distract the terrorists from making good on their specific threats. If they were operating on the same half-hour deadlines as the group aboard the *Tropic Princess,* then hostages would die before he reached the scene. More yet, if the police and soldiers ringing Bahia Matanzas slowed him down.

But he *would* find a way inside. And those he couldn't save, he would avenge.

Bolan made that a solemn promise to himself.

After fieldstripping and reassembling the Beretta, Bolan relaxed on the short bunk as best he could. Combat experience had taught him to sleep virtually anywhere, if someone wasn't shooting at him, and the tiny cabin of a submarine felt like the Ritz compared to some of Bolan's other bivouacs. Running submerged, it had no pitch and roll like surface ships, only a steady thrumming from the mighty engines that propelled it through the depths.

5

Cuba

It took a team of army engineers three-quarters of an hour to clear the access road. Muhunnad had done his best with what he had, telling his men to disable the engine of each car used in the makeshift barricade and to flatten all four tires. Muhunnad had not booby-trapped the vehicles, because he feared that killing soldiers early on would prompt the Cubans to attack with everything they had, ignoring any danger to the hostages.

In fact, although Muhunnad's men had done their utmost to prevent the cars from moving, short of torching them, it ultimately made no difference. An army crane had been dispatched and hoisted them aside, one by one, until the way was clear.

Now Muhunnad stood and waited in the hotel lobby, peering through a wall of lightly tinted glass, as a Jeep with three soldiers inside it approached. He had no doubt that there were others hiding on the grounds, surrounding the hotel block, weapons trained on every exit and window. And he smiled, knowing their efforts were in vain.

The Jeep drew closer, eased into the hotel's driveway and stopped. Its driver kept the engine idling, while his passengers stepped from the vehicle. One clearly was an officer, although Muhunnad did not recognize the Cuban army's rank insignia. The other was a common rifleman who stayed beside the vehicle, his weapon held at port arms while the officer approached the hotel's air-conditioned lobby.

Muhunnad went out to meet him. He supposed there were snipers hiding in the darkness all around him, any one of whom could drop him with a single shot, but if that happened, it would touch off an immediate bloodbath inside. Muhunnad trusted that the Cuban officer was wise enough to recognize that fact, if nothing else.

When they were ten or twelve paces apart, the officer stopped short and without introduction said, "You speak English."

Although he had not phrased it as a question, Muhunnad replied, "You know I do."

A nod confirmed it. "Why are you doing this?" the soldier asked.

Muhunnad frowned. "You've heard our various demands."

"Of course. I mean, why are you doing this in Cuba, when your target is America? We have no currency or influence in Washington. You must know this. Americans do not negotiate for hostages, much less in countries they refuse to recognize."

"It was convenient," Muhunnad said truthfully. "After Guantanamo, where was our hope of reaching the United States?"

His adversary seemed to see the sense in that, but plainly did not like Muhunnad's answer. "You have Cuban citizens inside," he said. "Employees. Common working people. If you're wise, you will release them now."

"Because Havana will not ransom them?"

"We share that trait, at least, with the Americans," the officer replied.

"Too bad. They'll have to die, then, I suppose."

"If you harm a Cuban citizen—"

"What will you do?" Muhunnad challenged. "Storm the place and make us kill them all? I doubt it, but if that is your intention, why delay? By all means, do it. Come ahead."

"You sound like an American," the officer declared.

"We've learned our lessons from them too."

"It is unfortunate that you must die, with all your men."

"We don't fear death," Muhunnad said. "Unlike a Communist, we cherish faith in Paradise. Why else have we come here, today?"

"I understand, now."

"Do you?"

"The demands are all for show. You mean to kill the hostages, no matter what is done," the officer replied.

"You said yourself, Americans do not negotiate."

"And if they did? What, then?"

"Then we would use their money and our liberated soldiers to pursue the great jihad."

"Your cause is hopeless. Spilling blood for its own sake is worse than foolishness. It's madness," the officer said.

"Then give the signal to your snipers. Take me down," Muhunnad said,

"There's time enough for that," the officer assured him. "We won't fire the first shot, but I promise you, we'll finish it."

"Good luck," Muhunnad said. "I hope you brought a lot of body bags."

Tropic Princess

EMRE MANDIRALI DIDN'T KNOW exactly where they were, but there was water all around the ship, with no land in sight. It troubled him, thinking about the sea and all the creatures swimming in it, some of them miles deep and strange beyond imagination.

Which of them would come to feed on him when he was dead? Or would he simply drift and sink into the freezing depths where sunlight never reached, pickled in brine, preserved forever by the cold?

Whatever lay in store for him, the Turk knew he would never see or spend the ransom Caspari had demanded for their hostages. The Americans would never pay, nor would they sit in front of television screens for nine days, watching people murdered every thirty minutes. They would try another rescue, intercede somehow.

Caspari's men were looking forward to it.

How else could they find their way to Paradise?

The fundamental weakness of a Western soldier was his own survival instinct. Western soldiers weren't afraid of killing, but they didn't want to die. Except in moments of extreme duress—as when a rare one threw himself atop a live grenade to save his comrades in the heat of battle—who among them even thought of dying for a cause?

There'd been no doubt in Mandirali's mind that he would die aboard the *Tropic Princess,* or perhaps when it went down, a thrashing minnow, swallowed and forgotten by the sea. Granted, he had been briefly disappointed following his liberation, when the nature of the mission was explained to him, but death had been a part of the equation from the moment he joined the struggle.

Countless others had already sacrificed themselves.

Now, it was his turn—or would be, soon.

Caspari's first deadline was rapidly approaching, and the cruise ship's passengers were growing tense. After the first rescue attempt and the execution of the first group of hostages, it had required the better part of ninety minutes to corral the rest and herd them into common areas where they could be controlled, watched constantly. The restaurants worked best, once the majority of exits had been chained and padlocked.

Now, one man could guard four hundred prisoners, as long as they were calm and cherished hopes of going home alive.

But when the steady, rhythmic killing started, anything could happen. Once the sheep ran out of hope…

The Turk glanced at his wristwatch—thirty-seven minutes left—and then surveyed the sullen faces ranged before him, people slumped at tables and in corners of the Mardi Gras Buffet, located on the Lido Deck. They had no food to keep them occupied, but there were toilets to his left, no exits from them other than the doors covered by Mandirali's mini-Uzi, and he let them make the short, humiliating trek two at a time.

When they lost hope and worked up nerve enough to rush him, Mandirali knew that he could not control them. Thirty-two rounds from his Uzi, firing ten per second, wouldn't stop four hundred raging hostages from ripping him apart and stomping him to death. With that in mind, he'd placed his hand grenades where they were plainly visible, their pins already loosened.

When they rushed him, it would be a massacre.

And Emre Mandirali would be on his way to his reward.

Cuba

GHULAM YAZID HAD SEEN the soldiers come and had watched them drive off, disappointed. Even though he couldn't hear what passed between their leader and Muhunnad, Yazid still knew the gist of it. The soldiers wanted Muhunnad to change his mind and beg for mercy, but Yazid's leader refused.

That meant the soldiers would be coming back.

But not to talk.

Yazid had been in similar situations, and had managed to escape. This time, he knew, there was no exit, no chance for escape.

Better to die fighting his enemies than squatting in a

cage somewhere, waiting for infidels to ask the same questions repeatedly.

It pleased Yazid greatly when Muhunnad selected him and two others—Bahram Parwana and Ishaq Uthman—to leave the hotel proper through a service entrance and patrol the grounds for lurking enemies. Although he barely knew the other two assigned to work with him, Yazid accepted them as members of Allah's Warriors, and as brothers in the one true faith.

What else was there?

They crept outside, Yazid leading, Parwana and Uthman following at two-minute intervals, creeping through an access tunnel they hoped any watchers outside might have missed. From the tunnel's exit, it was a short dash to the lush undergrowth of the resort's famous tropical garden.

No one fired on them there, but Yazid still remained on alert, creeping through the minijungle and taking special care to be quiet, advancing one painstaking step at a time. They carried no flashlights and spoke not a word, navigating by lights from the hotel block and those posted along the driveway.

The main attack, when it came, would come from that direction, Yazid thought.

Instead of fanning out and scouring the grounds for snipers, who were surely hidden at strategic points throughout, Yazid determined to surprise the soldiers when they came. With his companions, he picked out a place along the driveway where advancing cars were forced to slow for speed bumps and a guard booth, now abandoned with the red-and-white-striped gate arms raised.

Yazid and his companions were armed with AKSU rifles, stubby versions of the classic AK-74 with folding stocks and eight-inch barrels, barely twenty-seven inches long with the skeleton stocks extended. For all their small size, however, the AKSUs gave up none of their parent weapon's devastating firepower, spraying 5.56 mm rounds at a rate of eight hundred per minute.

Pockets heavy with spare 30-round magazines, the three guerrillas waited until revving engine sounds alerted them to danger drawing near. The military vehicles approached with headlights off, but some strategic genius failed to cut the resorts electric power, leaving the trucks and their passengers fully illuminated by pole lights spaced along the drive at hundred-foot intervals.

"Wait until I fire," Yazid told his companions.

As he spoke, he raised the AKSU to his shoulder, pressed his cheek against the metal stock and fixed its sights upon the point he had chosen for the bottleneck. He did not track his enemies, but rather let them come to him, flies blundering into the spider's web.

"So easy," Yazid whispered to himself. "So easy, now."

MARIA SANTOS WOULD'VE missed the skirmish if she had relied on public radio, but since she also carried an illegal scanner in her car, she learned about the firefight moments after it began.

The first reports were typically chaotic. Troops advancing on the main hotel had taken fire, had suffered casualties and had returned fire. Moments later, as she lit another cigarette, Santos learned that gunfire had disabled two army vehicles, killing at least one soldier and wounding several more. During one short, demented broadcast she heard automatic weapons firing in the background, punctuated by a scream.

She sat and listened, glancing at her dashboard clock more frequently than wisdom dictated, wishing Matt Cooper would arrive—or, better yet, that she would get a call on her cell phone, telling her the mission had been canceled. Leave her out of it entirely. Let her live in peace.

Or simply let her *live*.

Santos wanted no part of a shooting war, but there she sat,

already on the fringe of it. And if she went ahead with her assignment, guiding an American into the very battle zone, what would become of her?

More static crackled from the scanner, then a strained voice told her that the soldiers were retreating from Bahia Matanzas, dragging their wounded to safety, driving the vehicles that still remained to them, all under wicked and punishing fire.

The army—and the government at large—would be embarrassed now. Santos wondered how they would react, whether with caution or repressive violence. If the troops went back in force, stormed the resort, her job was done. She could meet Cooper on the beach, perhaps invite him for a classic Cuban breakfast at a small café she liked, then send him back to the United States.

Of course, that meant the loss of hostages—perhaps a major part of the hotel—before the terrorists were finally subdued. In short, a bloodbath.

Would the government care?

And when Matt Cooper arrived…what then?

Santos knew he had not been sent as a negotiator, to placate the terrorists and talk them into peaceably releasing hostages. As for his plans, what he might ask of her, she had no clue.

Go home, a small voice in her head suggested. Drive back to your flat, puncture one of the car's tires, and call to say you couldn't make it. Someone else would be assigned to deal with Cooper. Even on short notice, surely it was possible.

"I can't do that," she muttered, through a pale haze of tobacco smoke. "I won't."

She couldn't leave him stranded now, not when he'd come so far to help.

To kill, the small voice challenged her.

But maybe that was helping, too.

The government she served, despite its revolutionary roots,

denounced all acts of terrorism. Defining terrorism might be problematic, and she would have bet Havana's definition differed radically from Washington's, but crimes against the state, against the Cuban people, merited a stern response.

It that sense, she was serving on the side of law and order—even if she was committing treason in the process, by collaborating with the CIA.

A new voice on the scanner now revised the butcher's bill from Bahia Matanzas. Sniper fire had killed four soldiers, maybe five, and wounded eight or nine. The swift retreat, it seemed, had turned into a rout.

Her countrymen were dying. Others were still trapped in the hotel, under a threat of death.

Maria Santos scowled, thinking, *For that, you pay.*

Tropic Princess

"IT IS TIME," Caspari said. "Select ten hostages and bring them to the Sun Deck. Now."

Osman Zarghona bobbed his head and left the bridge with Ali Ben Kalil, a Palestinian survivor of the raid on Guantanamo Bay. Together, they descended two staircases to reach the Lido Deck. There, they found Emre Mandirali standing guard alone over a crush of restless passengers, inside the Mardi Gras Buffet.

None of the hostages were weeping yet, though some had tearstained faces. More would start to wail and moan, as soon as ten were chosen and extracted. Once Zarghona and Kalil departed with their prey, it would remain for Mandirali to control the rest by any means required.

"It's time," Mandirali said as they entered.

"Do you want to choose?" Zarghona asked him.

The Turk rose from his chair and moved among the hostages, secure knowing that Zarghona and Kalil would cover him. He paused at this table, then that one, speaking quietly in broken English. One by one, the first six of the chosen stood, some smiling for their loved ones, then moved toward the exit where Zarghona and Kalil stood waiting for them.

"Is it true?" a gray-haired woman asked Zarghona. "You're releasing us, to show good faith?"

Zarghona shrugged. Why not preserve the fiction, if it made his duty easier. "You are to be released," he said.

It wasn't quite a lie.

The seventh hostage Mandirali chose refused to leave the woman he was seated with—presumably his wife, although Zarghona thought there had to be twenty years between them. Mandirali showed good sense. Rather than provoke an incident, he allowed the younger woman to be number eight.

The last two were a portly, balding Chinese man, and a black man from the cruise ship's crew. Zarghona and Kalil directed them outside the restaurant, left Mandirali in his chair with ten less prisoners to guard and started back in the direction of the Sun Deck.

The stairs were treacherous, providing opportunities for prisoners to spring upon their captors if they dared. Zarghona sent Kalil ahead to watch the hostages as they were climbing, one by one, while he watched the rear. If anyone tried anything, all ten were in a cross fire, helpless to escape.

No one tried.

They reached the Sun Deck fifteen minutes after leaving the bridge.

The leading hostages stopped short when they saw the corpses sprawled in front of them. Zarghona thought they should have been removed before another batch was brought for execution, but the choice did not belong to him. When the selected captives started muttering and weeping, when they turned back toward the stairs, Zarghona and Kalil were there to stop them with their automatic weapons.

"To the rail," he ordered, raising his Kalashnikov and sighting down its barrel when they didn't move.

"You mean to kill us anyway," one of the male captives replied. He was an older man, his sandy hair salted with silver. "Why the fuck should we do anything you say?"

"You're right," Zarghona said, and shot him in the chest.

The others bolted toward the railing. Kalil pursued them, while Zarghona took his time. There was no need to run. They had nowhere to go.

When they were pressed against the Sun Deck's rail he fired again, strafing the line of them from left to right and back again. Kalil emptied his submachine gun, then reloaded it and was about to fire again, until Zarghona said, "Enough."

"Enough?"

"We need to dump them over," Zarghona said. "For the next time."

"Ah."

Together, one by one, they rolled and pitched the corpses overboard. The first man he had killed was heavy, but they dragged him to the rail, each gunman pulling on an arm, and tipped him over into darkness. There was nothing to be done about the blood.

"Better," Zarghona said. "Let's get back to the bridge."

Cuba

THE ZODIAC INFLATABLE RAFT was powered by an outboard motor, far from silent, that propelled Bolan through cresting breakers toward the beach.

It was a choppy ride, taxing his skill and strength to keep the Zodiac on course, but nothing like a long swim to the beach from the *Poseidon,* already submerging now, three-quarters of a mile offshore. This way, at least, he wouldn't be exhausted, soaked through to the skin and freezing if he found an ambush waiting for him on the beach.

It could be cops or soldiers, if the meet went bad. His money was on soldiers, since invasion of the country—even by a single man—fell under state security provisions. Then again, he guessed that there were varied strata of authority in Cuba, any one of which would gladly gun him down or clap him in a cell if he was caught.

But there were no gunmen in evidence as Bolan beached his craft and started dragging it ashore. Halfway across the sand, he saw a slender woman coming from the shadows to assist him, frowning by moonlight.

"Matt Cooper?" she inquired. Brognola hadn't bothered to provide a password, telling Bolan simply that the meet would work out, or it wouldn't.

"Right. I'm Cooper," Bolan said. "And you're Maria Santos?"

"*Sí.* I am."

"Okay. First thing, I need to get this out of sight."

"Of course."

She stooped and helped him haul the raft into the woods, above the high-tide line. Bolan concealed the boat as best he could, amidst lush ferns and grass. He cut no brush for camouflage, since it would simply brown and wither, serving to reveal the spot to anyone with careful eyes.

"You have a car?" he asked her.

"Come with me," she replied.

6

Cuba

Bolan didn't mind the woman driving. It was her car, her home territory, and it gave him time to study here while they discussed her plan.

"Scuba?" he asked, when she had briefly laid it out for him.

Talking around her unlit cigarette, waiting for the soft click of the dashboard lighter, she replied, "It gets you past the soldiers and the government patrol boats. None of them will see you, if you're careful on the beach. I know the perfect place to come ashore."

"Will there be landmarks I can spot at night, based on your diagram?"

The click came, and Santos spent a moment lighting up before she answered through a cloud of smoke. "I'm coming with you," she replied. "I've ordered gear for two."

"Hold on, now—"

"You have reservations? So do I," she challenged him. "But I don't know the underwater landmarks, can't describe them well enough to guide you safely. I can only show you."

"All right, then," he said. "You lead me to the beach, then turn around and split. How's that?"

"Do you speak Spanish?" she inquired. "Perhaps you need a translator."

"The men I'm looking for speak English," Bolan said. "At least, their leaders do. All their demands have been in English, and Canadians run the resort. Most of the guests speak English, and I'm betting on a fair proportion of the staff."

"But for the others—"

"When's the last time that you killed a man?" he interrupted.

"What?" The question startled her. "I…never."

"Right. In case you missed it, I'm not a negotiator or psychologist. I didn't come to open up a dialogue or stall for time. That's why we're stopping on the way for guns."

"And scuba gear," she said, forcing a smile. "I think you call it one-stop-shopping."

"Great. My point is that I'm going in to fight. The other side has at least eight men. Once they're neutralized, the hostages are safe. That's why I'm here."

"To neutralize these men," Santos said.

"Kill them, in other words."

"They'll be on full alert," she said, "now that the soldiers tried and failed. You need someone to watch your back."

Santos had already briefed him on the grim debacle of the military raid. She was correct about the blunder putting Bolan's enemies on red alert.

So what?

They would've been keyed up and revving from the moment that it started, likely from the time they broke out of Guantanamo. Somewhere along the way, he knew that they were bound to crash, but Bolan couldn't sit around and wait for that to happen.

There were deadlines running, with the emphasis on *dead*.

"To watch my back," he said, "I need a soldier like myself."

"You mean, a man."

"I mean professional. Someone who's actually fired a shot in anger would be helpful. Better yet, someone who's fought and lived to talk about it. Someone who has dirty hands and doesn't mind."

"I'm all you've got," Santos countered.

"In that case," Bolan said, "I'll try it on my own."

He didn't bother adding "No offense." Her feelings were irrelevant. The mission mattered. Nothing else.

"It's your decision," she replied. "But for the record, I believe you're making a mistake."

"So noted. How much farther is it to our stop?"

She took his hint, accelerating as she said, "Ten minutes, then another four kilometers to the resort."

"Are you expecting company?" he asked.

"Customers come and go, all hours of the day and night. Jesús provides a wide variety of services."

Bolan had the Beretta slung beneath his left arm, dagger in its sheath, and a large wad of money in his pocket. By one means or another, he would get the hardware he needed to complete his mission.

Bahia Matanzas

"DAMNED FOOLS!" Muhunnad said. "Now they have forced my hand."

Thirteen minutes remained on his first demand deadline, but the Cuban soldiers had left Muhunnad no choice. He had threatened retaliation in the event of a rescue attempt, and killing the attackers didn't count. In order to preserve his credibility, he had to spill more blood.

Not that it bothered him, but with the Cuban troops already agitated, spoiling for a fight, his next move might provoke another raid, this time in force.

So what?

His mission boiled down to protracted suicide, but the key

word was protracted. If he rushed it, brought the final conflagration on too soon, would he be counted as a failure? Would it all have been for naught?

Ridiculous.

The message had already been broadcast. Whatever followed, in whichever order the events occurred, his triumph was assured. Blame for the massacres would settle squarely on the White House, for its stubborn failure to negotiate.

Tabari stood beside him, waiting. He had done well with the soldiers, but his bloody work was not complete.

"Pick out five hostages," Muhunnad said, "and take them to one of the cottages you wired with plastic charges."

Tabari turned away to carry out his orders. He was a professional, although a Saudi, whom most Palestinians distrusted as a rule of thumb. His royal leaders catered to America, and while Tabari wouldn't live to see it, they would someday suffer retribution for their greed.

Meanwhile, Muhunnad and his men had work to do.

At his order, explosives had been placed in every third beach cottage, equipped with remote-control detonators. Muhunnad had conceived them as a first line of defense against attackers from the sea, or as diversions if the raiders came by land, but now one of the traps would serve a different purpose.

Tabari came back moments later, prodding two men and three women before him. Muhunnad surveyed the chosen hostages, then beckoned the Iranian, Cirrus Mehrzad, to join them.

To the hostages he said, "We have been attacked by Cuban soldiers, from the highway. I believe their next attempt will be amphibious. I'm placing you in one of the beach cottages, with guards, to make them reconsider."

"And if they attack?" one of the women asked.

"Bad luck for you."

"For God's sake—"

"Silence, infidel!" Muhunnad snapped. "If you prefer a bullet here and now, you can be easily replaced!"

The five stood silently before him, two of the selected women trembling and weeping. Neither of the men would meet his gaze.

"We stay with them?" Tabari asked in Arabic.

Muhunnad answered in the same tongue, "No, but make them think you'll be outside, then call me when you're out of range."

Tabari nodded, and Muhunnad saw Mehrzad smiling at him. He ignored it, standing ready with his weapon as the men took their hostages outside. A moment later, they were lost to sight, vanished among the trees and shadows on their short walk to the beach.

Muhunnad ran a hand along his belt and found the detonator, clipped beside his cell phone. Marvels of technology, he thought, and still they serve the timeless will of Allah.

By the time Tabari phoned him, Muhunnad supposed the deadline would have passed. He could achieve two objects with one touch of the remote-control detonator's red button. Let the infidels offshore watch and be horrified.

In fact, the bloodletting had only just begun.

SANTOS'S CONTACT WAS a forty-something man with oily hair, a round face and a beer gut over skinny legs. He ran a combination gas station and general store, with more room in the back than out in front. After a rapid-fire discussion with Santos in Spanish, and a long, suspicious look at Bolan, he admitted them to what he called his special showroom, where the value of the inventory far exceeded anything available to most customers.

Many of the weapons on display were Russian models, or knockoffs produced in former iron curtain countries and China, but there were exceptions. Bolan found a Steyr AUG assault rifle, fieldstripped it, and found nothing that should keep it from performing on demand. He filled a sack with magazines, the see-through plastic kind, and ample ammunition for his needs. Next up, a fair selection of grenades, including flash-bangs, antipersonnel and others, for the Steyr's built-in launcher. Keeping the swim in mind, he also bought an army-surplus body bag to keep his weapons dry on their submerged approach to the resort.

Bolan let Santos choose the scuba gear, but checked it out before he paid their host for anything. The tanks were full of air, at least according to the regulators, and the hoses didn't leak. Their simple weight belts, fins and masks all seemed to be in decent shape. Bolan had packed a wet suit when he heard that he'd be traveling aboard a submarine, and didn't ask Santos what she would be wearing on their swim.

When they were finished and the bill was paid, they carried the gear to the car and stowed it in the trunk. There would be hell to pay if they were stopped and searched by the police, but Bolan didn't let it bother him. So many things could still go wrong that adding one more to the list was hardly worth the effort.

Santos waited until they were back on the road to ask, "What are the explosives for?"

"I like to be prepared," Bolan replied.

"You're like a Boy Scout, eh?" She almost smiled. "I think there's more to it."

"The flash-bangs are for dealing with an adversary who has hostages. The rest, I'll have to wait and see."

"Unknown contingencies," she said, and finally produced the smile.

"How long have you been with the Company?" Bolan asked.

"Almost three years."

"It's risky for you," he said.

She shrugged. "We all do what we must."

"How much longer to our stop?" the Executioner asked.

In answer to his words, Santos turned into a narrow access road fronting the beach and killed her headlights, following the track by moonlight only for another hundred yards before she stopped and set the parking brake.

"We're here," she said. "Ready to swim?"

Bahia Matanzas

MUHUNNAD'S CELL PHONE WAS busy when Tabari called. He broke the link and turned back toward the cottage where he'd left the chosen hostages, some thirty yards away. Mehrzad stood several paces to his right, watching and waiting.

They were still too close for comfort, if the C-4 charges detonated, but Tabari couldn't leave the prisoners unsupervised. He'd ordered them to stay inside the cottage, warned them of dire consequences from nonexistent watchdogs if they poked their heads outside, but there was no way to secure the doors, either in front or facing the beach and sea beyond. Why wouldn't some of them try slipping out, if they were unobserved?

If circumstances were reversed, Tabari thought, he would've tried to kill his captors, or at least escape unseen while they were otherwise engaged. Only a foolish sheep sat waiting to be slaughtered by his enemies.

Though, granted, hostages were mostly sheep.

He tried Muhunnad's phone again and got another busy signal. They were late now, past the deadline, but he couldn't go back to the main hotel and leave the hostages to run away.

Send Mehrzad? What if something happened to him on his way back? Soldiers could waylay him on the path and kill him, unknown to Tabari, while Tabari stood and waited in the shadows all night.

Was something wrong at the hotel?

Behind him, at the main hotel, roughly twelve hundred prisoners were ranged against six gunmen, with himself and Mehrzad absent. Even with their weapons loaded to capacity, assisted by some miracle that let each bullet find a fatal mark, Muhunnad's soldiers could kill no more than two hundred of their hostages before the other thousand trampled them to bloody pulp.

Of course, psychology was more than half the battle, cowing prisoners into accepting their own helplessness, their worthlessness, breaking them down.

But if that failed…

Tabari got through on his third attempt, discarding the amenities to blurt out, "I tried twice before. Your telephone rang busy."

"I was talking to the Cubans," Muhunnad replied, sounding remarkably at ease. "They beg us to do nothing rash." His laughter was a rasp, grating across Tabari's nerves.

"The prisoners are in the cottage," Tabari said.

"Are you clear?"

"We couldn't leave them unsecured," he said.

"Fall back, then," Muhunnad ordered. "You have ten seconds."

"Come on!" Tabari snapped at Mehrzad, turning from the cottage as he spoke, retreating at a jog along the garden path. He reckoned one long stride per second, each one taking him another yard from the cottage where the infidels stood waiting, staring out to sea and either hoping for, or dreading, rescue by the Cuban military.

Eight strides. Nine. Ten. Clearly he'd miscalculated, and—

The blast behind Tabari was a thunderclap, its echoes rolling out to sea and battering against the tall block of hotel rooms farther inland. The percussive shock wave staggered him. Tabari ducked, fearing a storm of shrapnel, but the trees around him took the worst of it, catching discarded shingles, wooden slats and chunks of plaster, stuffing ripped from furniture—and something wet.

Tabari got his balance back and kept on running, didn't turn to see if Mehrzad was behind him in the smoky darkness, or if he had fallen with a piece of drywall in his skull.

A moment later, the Iranian was there beside him, grinning like a child when school was canceled early for a holiday. "You hear them, brother?" he inquired, aiming an index finger at the dark trees overhead. "It's raining infidels."

"I'M TELLING YOU," James Foreman said, "they're going to kill all of us, if we just sit around and wait."

He was a certified accountant from Toronto, made his living at a desk five days a week, but Foreman was a weekend athlete, still in decent shape at forty-two, an autumn hunter who enjoyed his guns and stalking big game in the snowy woods.

"Says you," a slim, red-faced casino dealer from Vancouver answered Foreman. "What do you know?"

There were seven of them—four men and three wives, including Foreman's—huddled together in the southwest corner of the hotel lobby, near the elevators that had been deactivated by their captors. All of them were scared, but none had panicked—yet.

"I know that no one in the States is going to negotiate with these assholes," Foreman replied. "They wouldn't bargain for Americans. What do you think they'll do for us?"

The others stared at him, so he pressed on. "I know the people they marched outside are dead by now, or will be, very soon. I know that's just round one."

"You and your deadline shit," the dealer spit at him. "You heard it on the TV, so it must be true? Give me a break."

"Christ, will you look around and *think,* for just a second?"

Foreman challenged. "Remember in the seventies, the airline hijackings that used to happen every week or so?"

"I wasn't born yet," a slender, bleached-blond trophy wife said.

"My *point* is that they always set a deadline. Putting heat on the authorities, making them run and fetch. Except there'll be no fetching this time. Cuban cops can't help us without touching off a bloodbath, and I guaran-fucking-tee you that the Yanks don't give a shit what happens here tonight, as long as they save face."

"You make this sound like it's a game," the second woman said.

"Damn right, because it *is* a game," Foreman told her. "It's called Survival of the Fittest, and we're all playing, whether you like it or not. They've already killed soldiers. We all heard the gunfire. You think it was fireworks? Some kind of a party? This isn't—"

The blast was horrendous, a physical blow that rattled the hotel's plate glass windows and made half the people confined in the lobby emit little squeals.

"What's that?" the blonde demanded.

"That," Foreman said, "was the end of five good people picked at random for a human sacrifice. All right? We have another thirty minutes now, before these fuckers come around and pick ten more. That is, if we sit here and let them."

"What are you suggesting?" asked a slender British man from London, salt-and-pepper hair combed back from a high forehead.

"We either stand and fight like human beings, or we die like cattle in a goddamned slaughterhouse," Foreman said.

"Fight, how?" the dealer asked, going pale.

"I have a thing or to in mind," Foreman replied, and quietly began to sketch his desperate plan.

"WHAT'S THIS PLACE CALLED?" Bolan asked Santos, as they started to unload their scuba gear.

"Bahia de Sangre," she said.

"We're starting from the Bay of Blood? Terrific," Bolan said. "How did it get that name?"

"At sundown," she said, "all the water here is painted brilliant crimson. Someone in the old days saw it and decided that it looked like blood."

"Any sharks?" Bolan asked.

"There may be sharks or barracuda," she said. "Anything is possible. I worry more about patrol boats."

"Right."

"Still, if you follow me, they shouldn't see us. They'll be focused on the hotel and the gardens, the beach cottages, the—"

Bolan saw Santos flinch as an explosion echoed over land and sea. It came from somewhere to the west.

"Sounds like the party went ahead without us," Bolan said.

He waited for another moment, half expecting gunfire, more explosions, sounds of battle joined. When nothing came, Santos asked him, "So, what do you think it was?"

A quick glance at his watch by moonlight made him frown. "A deadline passing," he replied. "They've started killing hostages."

"We're too late, then," she said.

"Not if they stay on schedule," he reminded her. "That gives us twenty-nine minutes and counting, for the next group."

"Who are these people?"

"Predators." He tried the scuba mouthpiece, found the flow of canned air unimpeded. "Are you ready?"

"Yes," she answered. "And you follow me, correct?"

He nodded. "You're the guide."

Santos, in a one-piece bathing suit and scuba gear, led the

way into the gently rolling surf. Bolan trailed behind her with
the rubber body bag that held his mobile arsenal.

Santos wore a semiauto pistol tied to her weight belt, inside
a plastic bag with two spare magazines. Bolan assumed it was
a mere security precaution, but he took a moment to repeat
himself, before they were submerged, unable to communicate.

"You get me to the beach and then turn back. Agreed?"

Removing her mouthpiece, she answered, "I thought we
already discussed this."

"We did," he granted. "I'm confirming it."

"You shouldn't be so…what's the word in English? Anal."

And with that she left him, wading out until the water
reached her waist, then covered her breasts. Mouthpiece
firmly in place, she ducked below the surface and was gone,
while Bolan followed.

Moonlight stayed with them as they started swimming west.

The Executioner was in a new world now, but only tem-
porarily. And he knew it could he as hostile as the one he'd
left behind.

7

Where's a spear gun when you need one? Bolan asked himself in vain.

As they swam, Bolan behind Santos, a scowling barracuda kept keeping pace to starboard. But there was no attack. Perhaps the fish mistook him for a shark or other, larger predator—which, to some extent, would have been correct.

Bolan reckoned he had air enough remaining in his tanks for another half hour, but it shouldn't take that long to reach their destination, if their calculation of the distance was correct.

A low-pitched rumbling in the water answered Bolan's silent question. Santos stopped and turned to face him, pointing with her left hand, away from shore.

It took a second, but he got the point.

Cuban patrol boats, trolling off the coast of the resort, to watch for fleeing fugitives.

A nod from Bolan put her back in motion, swimming westward. Bolan followed, towing his bag of weapons and explosives.

Almost there, and soon the killing would begin.

Tropic Princess

"WHAT'S THAT BLIP, off to the west?" Caspari asked the radar operator.

"I'm not sure," the man answered. "There's no visual outside, and it's retreating."

From the cruise ship's bridge, Caspari had a 360-degree view of the ocean surrounding the *Tropic Princess*. Staring westward, past the bright lights of the ship, he could see nothing in the darkness stretching off to the invisible horizon.

"Does the image indicate a boat or aircraft?" Caspari asked.

Turning back, he caught the radar operator making eye contact with Captain Bateman, plainly hoping that the skipper of the *Tropic Princess* might provide an answer. Lunging toward the radar terminal, Caspari shoved the muzzle of his Uzi underneath the operator's chin.

"I ask a question, *you* respond!" he ordered.

"Air-aircraft," the frightened sailor stammered. "I can't tell what kind, but from the quick reversal there, I'd guess a chopper."

"So, a helicopter first approaches, then turns back?"

"Could be the media," Bateman said. "Maybe they want to film us, but the navy called them off."

"Whose navy?" Caspari asked.

"We're approaching the Bahamas now, as you instructed," Bateman said. "Not close enough to see them, yet, but we're within their waters."

"Safe from the Americans, at least," Zarghona said.

"Don't count on that," Caspari snapped. "Go now, and check the others. Make sure all of them are still in place."

"Of course."

Zarghona turned to leave the bridge, then hesitated as Caspari said, "No, wait! Go back and check the water first."

"The water?"

"Check the ocean. There's a chance this phantom airship may have left a present for us," Caspari said. "I don't like surprises."

"What surprise?" Zarghona asked. "What present?"

"Do not question me!" Caspari raged. "Go now, and do as you are told!"

Zarghona left without another word or backward glance. Caspari wished that he could follow, making sure his surly new subordinate obeyed directions and did not slip off for coffee in the galley.

Damn the man for questioning authority, when their success required a strong united front against their captives and the world at large.

In fact, Caspari didn't know what kind of rude surprise he was expecting from their enemies, but there was something in the air. He knew that Washington would let deadline after deadline slip away, the corpses piling up. They wouldn't pay, wouldn't negotiate—but they would act.

Somehow.

The radar blip reminded him of their encounter with the U.S. Navy helicopter, earlier. The *Tropic Princess* was outside American waters now, but did that make any difference to a nation that kidnapped terrorist suspects from foreign countries and called it "rendition," shipping them off to third-party nations for "strenuous interrogation" banned by America's own Constitution?

Soldiers are coming, Caspari thought, feeling it with certainty.

"You, tell me," he demanded of the radar operator, "are there any boats behind us?"

"Boats?" The sailor seemed confused.

"You heard me! Boats behind us, following. Are there?"

"No ships," the operator said. "They'd show up on the screen. I can't say, as to smaller craft. Speedboats, whatever, wouldn't leave a signature."

Cursing bitterly, Caspari palmed his cell phone, keyed the speed-dial number shared by telephones his soldiers carried. When he had all on the line, he said, "We may be boarded soon, by enemies. Be vigilant. Stand by to execute the hostages on my command."

THE NAVY SEALS FIRED grappling hooks and lines from the Zodiac rafts, up toward the railing and lights of the cruise ship that towered above them. Three out of four made solid contact on their first attempt, men scrambling up the lines hand-over-hand while their companions in the fourth boat tried again and got it right the second time.

Like spiders they ascended, scrabbling in the dark. With their weapons slung and holstered, all were helpless on the lines while they were climbing. Dead if one of the terrorists discovered them and started firing at them from the rail.

But no one did.

It puzzled Captain Ernest Ryan, but he let it go, too wired on pure adrenaline to look a gift horse in the mouth. The brass said there were only seven shooters on the whole huge ship, most of them likely guarding hostages and crew, so maybe they were spread too thin to watch the ocean. Maybe they had missed the Zodiacs approaching, running underneath the cruise ship's radar.

Maybe.

Or, they could've set a trap onboard. Maybe his SEALs weren't spiders after all, but flies.

To hell with maybes, he thought.

Ryan issued whispered orders to his men, divided them in four-man teams. One starboard, one to port, along the open deck. One to the bridge, and one to clear the engine room below. Two staring on the Lido Deck and working downward, bow to stern, checking the common areas where hostages were likely to be held in groups.

He didn't tell them what to do with any captured terrorists, because there'd be none. All on board had to be eliminated, neutralized before one of them had a chance to detonate the charges lurking somewhere below the waterline.

And if there were no charges? Then, what?

They would find out later, when the threat had passed and those responsible were body-bagged.

Ryan, as their commander, led the team that would assault the bridge. He'd seen a dossier on Captain Arnold Bateman, knew that he would recognize the cruise ship's skipper when they met. He didn't know the other officers by name, but photos of them had been passed among his SEALs, in case the hostiles traded clothes with any member of the crew, to gain an edge when it was killing time.

Ryan was first in line as they went up the last companion-way to reach the ship's bridge. He knew the layout, had seen photographs and diagrams of every deck and each significant onboard facility. They'd even studied photos of the several types of staterooms, just in case.

The bridge was forty feet by sixty, glassed in all around, so that the duty officers could watch for anything from rogue waves to a school of flying fish. Aside from polarized and lightly tinted windows, they had all the latest instruments for navigation and communication—not that it had done them any good.

Old-fashioned evil had still managed to sneak up on them and make them prisoners.

Ryan was nearly there. He paused, three steps before his head and shoulders would be visible to officers and shooters on the bridge. A glance back at his men assured him they were as ready as they'd ever be.

He raised his head and peered in through the tinted glass, across the lighted bridge. He saw Bateman standing with a man beside him and an Uzi submachine gun jammed beneath his chin. The gunman had a cell phone in his free hand and was speaking urgently into the mouthpiece.

He charged toward the nearest entrance to the bridge and shouting to his men as they came up behind him, "Go! Go! Go!"

FARID AZIMA WAS ASHAMED. His feeble body had betrayed him, nearly rendered him unconscious in his tiny cabin while his comrades went about their business on the *Tropic Princess.* More than once, in his delirium, he'd heard the cell phone chirping at him, urgently demanding his attention, but the stunning waves of nausea had forced him to ignore it.

How could anyone have conversations on the telephone when his entire digestive system was about to exit through his mouth? Could anyone expect him to go trotting belowdecks with his satchel of explosives, running here and there as if his stomach wasn't twisted into agonizing knots?

Now, hours later, he felt somewhat better, and the cell phone, too long silent by his pillow, had begun to chirp again. Fearing the worst—Sohrab Caspari's scathing torrent of abuse, richly deserved—Azima fumbled with the telephone and brought it to his ear. He did not have to fake the pain or dizziness that left him nearly breathless.

"Yes? Hello?"

"Farid?" It was, undoubtedly, Caspari's voice.

"Yes, I'm sorry. I've been—"

"Silence! Listen to me! There are soldiers on the ship. You understand me?"

"Soldiers? Where? I—"

"You must detonate the charges now!"

"The charges? Yes, I will, but—"

The line went dead.

Azima struggled to his feet, the pungent odor of himself almost enough to start another round of vomiting. Somehow, this time, he managed to control his gag reflex when he bent to clutch the gym bag filled with C-4 charges that he'd left beside his narrow bed.

Soldiers aboard the ship!

They'd likely find and kill him long before he reached his target, in the engine room—assuming he could still remember how and where to find it.

And if the soldiers intercepted him, then what?

The blocks of plastic in his gym bag were unarmed. As they were now, without their detonators, they could readily be tossed into a fire or used as clay for children's modeling.

Azima sat, opened the bag and started arming one square block of C-4 at a time. He had a trigger mechanism, like a pager, in his pocket, ready to ignite the blasting caps once they were primed and seated, each in its respective plastic charge.

The job took five full minutes, during which time he expected soldiers to attack and storm his cabin. When they didn't come, Azima gained confidence. Closing the bag, he stepped to the cabin door and opened it, peered out into the empty corridor beyond, and drew a pistol as he left his stateroom.

Now, if he could only find the engine room, he should be fine—until the moment he blew himself to smithereens and sank the giant ship that had tormented him and made him fail his comrades, like the weakling that he was.

Pure rage and hatred—at himself, the *Tropic Princess,* those who wished to stop him and prevent his entry into Paradise—kept Azima on his feet as he proceeded down and down, into the bowels of the cruise ship.

Washington, D.C.

HAL BROGNOLA RETURNED to his office, horrified by what he'd just learned and the rest of the world would soon know.

He picked up the remote control and brought his smallish office TV set to life. It was already set on CNN, no need for channel surfing.

"…sinking, even as we speak now, Adrianna. I don't know how much of this you're getting in the studio, but—"

They were getting all of it, and it was terrible.

The camera had a bird's-eye view of a scene rivaling the worst in Brognola's long experience.

The *Tropic Princess* wallowed on its port side like a dying whale, the stern awash, bow rising slowly from the water. When it hit the vertical, Brognola thought, before it finally went down, the cruise ship would resemble a gigantic dorsal fin, a marker for the biggest, baddest shark that ever lived.

"…no lifeboats visible, so far, but there appear to be small objects—are those *rafts?* I don't seen anyone aboard them—smallish boats of some kind floating empty near the stern, where—"

The Zodiacs, Brognola thought.

The small inflatables weren't sinking yet, though he supposed the suction of the cruise ship, when it finally deep-sixed, would take them down, as well. Since they were floating now, it meant no one had riddled them with bullets when the would-be saviors made their move.

As for the fact that they were empty, the big Fed refused to speculate on what that meant. Suppose the SEALs who had piloted the rafts all got aboard the *Princess* without being spotted by their enemies. So, what? It was as clear as day that something had gone tragically, irrevocably wrong, or else the goddamned ship wouldn't be sinking live, on international TV.

"…see no one in the water so far, Adrianna. Normally, if you recall the shipwrecks that we've covered in the past, it's common to see swimmers in the water, even if there are no lifeboats. We—"

Brognola muted it. The visual was grim enough, without insipid commentary from a talking head who really didn't give a damn who died or walked away from any given tragedy, as long as he or she got airtime.

Brognola sat riveted, unblinking, as he watched the great ship die. And they were right again, goddamn it. He saw no one in the water. No one swimming, thrashing, floating for their lives.

Where were they?

Some of them were dead, of course. That was a given. When the rescue team had gone aboard, it had to mean a fire-fight somewhere on the ship. Given the choice of battling trained commandos or slaughtering unarmed civilians, most terrorists would take the cheap shot every time.

But none of that would sink the *Tropic Princess*.

So, there *had* been plastic charges, after all. Brognola couldn't think of any other explanation for the images that filled his screen. The ship was sinking. Explosive charges blown below the waterline had done what he was seeing.

The only question left was whether there would be survivors, or if the *Tropic Princess* would go down with all hands still aboard.

Forty-two hundred, give or take.

Brognola cursed and reached for the telephone.

8

Bahia Matanzas

Bolan knew the patrol boats were closer, though he still couldn't see them. They churned the offshore waters, trolling back and forth at least a couple of them covering the posh resort's expanse of private beach.

Unless his ears and other senses were deceiving him, the boats were moving faster, revving their engines as they made their endless passes up and down the coastline. He wasn't sure what that meant—whether soldiers on the boats were simply bored, or they had been alerted to some action in the offing—but he knew the greatest danger to himself and to his mission, from the troops, would be the moment when he went ashore.

After the hours of frustration and the loss of life, including several men in uniform, the Cuban soldiers would be tickled to spot a human target on the beach and give it everything they had. Framed by their spotlights, Bolan wouldn't last ten seconds in the open, flayed by an incoming storm of automatic fire.

Santos had that angle covered, so she claimed. There was supposed to be a small inlet, east of the tourist beach, where jagged rocks and mangrove trees came right down to the water's edge. With any luck, the two of them could go ashore there, Bolan to continue onward, while Santos rested long enough to brave the swim back to her waiting car.

Simple…unless the soldiers had it covered, waiting to surprise whoever they could catch in their gunsights.

Granted, they'd be expecting someone to break out of the resort, not sneak inside, but any unexplained or unexpected movement on the shore would draw their eyes, their searchlight beams, their bullets.

Ahead, he saw Santos veer off course and toward the shoreline, forty feet away. Bolan did likewise, slowing as he saw her head and shoulders break the surface, then her lean and shapely figure vanished from the sea in front of him.

A moment later, the Executioner found himself among the roots of a great mangrove tree, with smooth stones underfoot. He surfaced cautiously, turning to scout the sea for gunships cruising past, but there were none in sight. He heard them still, but farther west.

"Hurry!" Santos urged from her place atop a seaside boulder.

Bolan scrambled up the makeshift ladder of the mangrove roots, dragging his arsenal behind him in the rubber body bag. Even if dampness had intruded, they had not been underwater long enough to foul his weapons or do damage to the ammunition and grenades.

Without the ocean's buoyancy, the bag regained its normal weight. He shouldered it without complaint and scrambled up beside Santos, then pushed inland, until he was shielded by the mangrove from whatever prying eyes might seek them out. In another moment, Bolan felt Santos kneeling at his side.

"This is a part of the resort?" he asked, confirming what she'd told him earlier.

"It is. Eight hundred acres, none of it devoted to the Cuban people."

Bolan let that pass and asked, "Which way to the hotel, again?"

She pointed northwest, saying, "That way. There are paths you can follow, when you've cleared the beach. I could—"

"Forget it," Bolan cut her off. "I'll find them."

Swiftly, without taking off his wet suit, Bolan slipped into his shoulder holster, buckled the commando dagger to his leg, then draped himself with bandoliers of ammunition and grenades. He checked the pistol and the Steyr AUG, finding both weapons dry and fully functional.

"You're going back now," Bolan told the woman.

Dutifully, she bobbed her head. "How will I find you, for the ride back to your boat?" she asked.

"Stay with your car, and I'll find you," Bolan replied. "If I'm not there by sunrise, pack it in and leave. That means—"

"I know." Her turn to cut him off. "Don't say it, please. *Hasta la vista,* then," she said.

"Later," he echoed, and without a backward glance proceeded inland, merging with the darkness.

THE DEATH THROES OF the *Tropic Princess* made a pretty spectacle on television, shot from every angle airborne cameras could achieve with modern video technology. Asim Ben Muhunnad exulted at the images displayed before him, but the great ship's final disappearance underwater also warned him that his time was near.

I don't have long to live, Muhunnad thought, and it surprised him somewhat that the notion neither pleased nor frightened him. For all his preparation, all his training and the endless lectures on the joys of Paradise that waited for a Muslim martyr, Muhunnad felt oddly distant and detached.

Behind him, in the rear part of the lobby, he could hear soft muttering among the hostages. One of his men shouted for silence without being told to give the order, and the prisoners stopped whispering, but they would soon begin again.

Why not? What did they have to lose?

The sinking of the *Tropic Princess,* broadcast at Muhunnad's order on the lobby's giant television, told them that this game was deadly serious. The wiser of them might already know that they were doomed, though personal experience had taught Muhunnad that hope often survived irrationally, even in the face of graphic evidence that should discourage it.

Still, he was worried now, about the prisoners.

If they organized somehow, if they attacked en masse, it was a given that his soldiers would be overwhelmed. There might not even be a chance to detonate the plastic charges he had planted at strategic points around the grand hotel, to bring its tons of steel and concrete crashing down upon their heads.

What difference does it make? Muhunnad asked himself.

Kill a hundred or a thousand, it was all the same to Allah, who judged warriors by intent as much as the results they managed to achieve. According to the scripture he'd been taught from childhood, one who drew a sword against the enemy but died before he had a chance to strike still had a place reserved in Paradise.

Muhunnad had already done a great deal more than that, even before he led the raid on Camp X-Ray. Whatever he accomplished now, at Bahia Matanzas was—how did they say it in America?

Gravy. The frosting on the cake.

Why was it always food, with the Americans? he wondered. Another symbol of their gluttony, perhaps?

The whispering among his prisoners had started up again. Three tables in the back—or was it four?—the farthest from the lobby's broad front windows where Muhunnad stood.

Perhaps he should approach them, smiling, then shoot two or three of them without another warning. Would that finally convince them that his orders had to be obeyed explicitly? Or should he choose his next victims from among the talkers when another deadline passed with no response from Washington?

Muhunnad checked his watch. Nine minutes left.

He smiled. Tabari saw it and looked puzzled, glancing toward the television screen that seemed to be the center of Muhunnad's focus. CNN had gone to split screen now, one of their blow-dried talking heads pontificating on the left side of the screen, while searchlights scanned an empty, restless ocean on the right.

Tabari frowned and shrugged, as if to ask, What's funny? Muhunnad could only shake his head, the smile still plastered on his face.

I'm ready now, he thought, and felt the strength of Allah welling inside him.

It was true.

Whatever happened next, Asim Ben Muhunnad was ready to confront his fate.

"NEXT ONE OF THEM who comes back here," James Foreman said, half-whispering, "I'm grabbing him."

Irene, his wife of nineteen years, gaped at him with a shocked expression on her face. "Are you insane?" she asked.

"Look at them," Foreman gritted. "Most of them look like someone's had them in a dungeon for the last five years. That little prick with the Kalashnikov keeps yawning like he's half asleep."

"They still have guns," the Vancouver dealer said.

"Sure," Foreman replied. "But if we take out one or two of them, then we'll have guns. See how they like it, then."

"You and your guns," he wife said, digging painted fingernails into his forearm. "Will you listen to yourself, for God's sake? These are terrorists. They kill people. It's not just paper targets at the shooting range, one Sunday every month or two."

"I did military service," he reminded her. "I know my way

around assault rifles. And yes, Irene, they're killers. That's exactly why we have to make a move while we still can. You saw what happened on that ship. You know what happened to the people they took out of here. They're killing us already. How long do you want to wait? Until it's our turn?"

The dealer leaned in closer. "If we start something—"

"It started when they took us prisoner," Foreman replied. "Do you not get that? Is there any doubt left in your mind that they intend to kill us all?"

To that, there was no answer from the others at his table. Foreman saw the people at two other nearby tables listening, pretending not to, some nodding in his direction while they spoke softly among themselves.

"All right," he said, as if the dealer had agreed with him. "The only question left is whether you want to sit here and be a good boy, help the bastards kill you without causing any trouble for them, or if you have nerve enough to fight."

The dealer's shoulders slumped. "I wasn't in the army like you were, okay? I haven't ever fired a gun. What kind of help is that?"

"Follow my lead when shit starts happening," Foreman said. "They don't know your level of experience, and they don't need to know. We take it one step at a time."

"I'm with you," said a third man. "I was in the Navy, never did much small-arms training, but I try to stay in shape. Karate and whatever."

"Perfect," Foreman answered.

"Guess I'm in," the fourth man said. "It's not much, but they missed my pocketknife when they were rousting us. Only a three-inch blade, but still—"

"Still something," Foreman eagerly agreed, anxious to keep their fighting spirits up. "Now, what we need to do is get one of them over here and close enough to grab, but only one.

No big disturbance. Just a little something that will make one come around and tell us to shut up, something like that."

"Too risky," the dealer said, looking sour.

"Then stay out of it," Foreman replied through gritted teeth. "And stay the hell out of our way."

BOLAN WAS CONSCIOUS of the time, could hear the numbers running in his head and feel those precious seconds slipping through his fingers, but he didn't rush his move toward the hotel. With soldiers dead and hostages already sacrificed on deadline, it was clear his adversaries knew their business, and they wouldn't hesitate to pick him off if he got sloppy.

Moving through the darkness, shunning asphalt trails that would have made his transit quicker, Bolan watched for trip wires, snares, or any other traps that might prevent him getting close enough to help the hostages. He only had to let his guard down for an instant, and—

He heard the soft purr of a zipper sliding down and froze in midstride, with his Steyr angled toward the sound. Two heartbeats passed, and Bolan was about to second-guess himself, call it an insect's whirring rather than a human-generated sound, and then his ears picked out the sound of running water.

And a sigh.

Somebody's on a bladder break, he thought.

But who?

For all he knew, there might be Cuban soldiers on the grounds, keeping the terrorists contained. Or, maybe one of them had come in on his own, seeking revenge for buddies killed in the ill-conceived frontal assault.

Either way, Bolan had to find out who was watering the garden.

He crept forward, moving silently and following the sounds to their source. A moment later, he was looking at the profile of a slender, dark-skinned gunman in civilian clothes, just zipping up his fly.

And Bolan knew that face from photos he'd been shown at the Farm—Mahmood Tamwar, one of the three Afghanis liberated in the raid on Camp X-Ray.

Tamwar had a short Kalashnikov, the AKSU model, slung across his left shoulder, its muzzle pointed toward the ground. Spare magazines protruded from the tight hip pockets of his denim pants, which rode low on his hips. If he was carrying a pistol, Bolan couldn't see it from his present vantage point.

The wiry rifleman half turned, showing his back to Bolan, giving him the opening he needed. The Executioner drew his knife and went at Tamwar in a rush, encircling the man's throat with his left arm and twisting backward, to the left, while he stamped down with his right foot behind the terrorist's right knee.

That action stunned Tamwar and bared his throat to Bolan's blade, the razor edge rising to meet him as his body slumped in Bolan's grasp. He shuddered, thrashing as the knife sheared through flesh and cartilage.

Bolan held the shooter while he died, keeping the knife well-buried in his throat to stifle any warning cry that might escape. They were alone, as far as Bolan knew, but why take any chances?

When the final tremor passed from Tamwar's dangling body, Bolan dragged him to a clump of ferns and left him there. He didn't take the dead man's weapon, reckoning that all of his remaining enemies were armed, and that another rifle wouldn't help them even if they found it.

He had never seen a man fire two Kalashnikovs at once, and didn't think that record would be broken here, this night.

One down. Seven to go.

SARSOUR IBN TABARI checked his wristwatch, vowing to himself that he would personally flay Tamwar if he had not returned from his assigned patrol within the next ten minutes. Granted, there had been no deadline specified for Tamwar's walk around the grounds of the resort, but he'd been told to hurry, which Tabari thought meant the same thing in any language.

So much for Afghanis.

As a Saudi, although not a member of the royal line, Tabari recognized a certain arrogance within himself that generally served him well. While other freedom fighters might have trouble with their nerves in crisis situations, like the present one, Tabari often took the prize for sheer audacity. In fact, he thought that *he* should have been chosen as a leader of the raid against Guantanamo, but that was now a moot subject.

As yet another deadline neared, he called that ancient history.

Tabari had dispatched Mahmood Tamwar to scout the nearby grounds because he feared the Cuban soldiers might be sneaking back to try another raid, regain some face after the beating they'd received last time. He understood the macho mindset, knew that it was not restricted to the Latin races, and had thought it best to guard against surprises, now that they were in the final stages of their plan.

In one respect, perhaps, it made no difference. They were supposed to sacrifice themselves, along with all the hostages, to shock America and horrify the world at large. It hardly mattered then, in concrete terms, whether the killing started with an army raid or passage of an arbitrary deadline, but Tabari also understood that in this age of global media, appearances were everything.

So, he had sent Tamwar outside to have a little look

around—not scour every acre of the huge resort, flip every stone, or beat each bush.

And now, the lazy goat was running late.

Tabari could've used his cell phone, but he didn't want the soldiers massed outside to overhear his conversation with Tamwar. They might already know one of the shooters was outside of the hotel, but if they didn't, then Tabari didn't plan to tip them off.

In retrospect, he wished that every member of their team had been equipped with tracking tags, so that their where-abouts and movements could be monitored. It would have been a cheap fix for a major problem, but the brainstorm came too late, as they so often did.

Now, even as he harbored mounting anger toward his irre-sponsible subordinate, Tabari made a mental list of mishaps that could be responsible for Tamwar's tardiness.

First possibility: the lazy fool had parked himself some-where and drifted off to sleep. Tabari viewed Afghanis as a lazy race in general, and would not put it past Tamwar to steal time for a nap when he had duties to perform.

Worse yet, he might have found himself a stash of alcohol. Such pleasures were forbidden by the tenets of Islam, but many self-styled Muslims treated Allah's binding and eternal laws as mere suggestions for behavior on the earthly plane, devoid of any consequences for a violation.

Then, although it strained credulity, there might have been some kind of accident. Perhaps Tamwar had fallen, or been injured otherwise—but where, and how? Surely, unless he was unconscious or had lost his eyesight, he could find his way back to the huge hotel from any point on the resort.

The final possibility was that Mahmood Tamwar no longer lived. He had run into trouble of the human kind during his tour of the grounds, and he had come off second-best. In which case, he would not be coming back, and the remainder of his team might never know his fate.

And would they care?

Tabari wouldn't miss the rude Afghani, might even forget him as the final hours of his own life ticked away, but it might help the team to know who'd killed him.

Cuban soldiers? Their security police?

Tabari checked his watch again, cursed bitterly and glowered at the clutch of hostages still whispering together, in the southwest corner of the hotel lobby. Soon, he had to inform Muhunnad that Tamwar had not returned.

But first, perhaps, a little discipline would lift his spirits and restore his fighting zeal.

Working his way across the lobby toward the huddled chatterboxes at the rear, Tabari found his smile.

AT FIRST, MARIA SANTOS thought the body that she'd nearly stumbled over might be Cooper's. Only when the first wild panic-rush was past and she could breathe again, did she observe the obvious—the clothes were wrong.

In place of Cooper's wet suit, with its shoulder holster, ammunition bandoliers and knife strapped to his leg, this prostrate figure wore a baggy cotton shirt and denim trousers. She removed two rifle magazines from his hip pockets, tucked them underneath her belt and claimed the rifle he no longer needed for herself.

It was a short Kalashnikov, identical in all but size to those used by the Cuban military and police. Santos had not fired one, but she knew the rough mechanics of it and felt better with the stubby weapon in her hands. Its seven pounds of metal and explosive power reassured her, standing in the dark alone.

Before she left, Santos took another moment to discover how the rifleman had died. She steeled herself to roll the body over, saw the gaping ruin of his throat and closed her eyes, imagining Matt Cooper savaging the dead man with his blade.

Who else could it have been?

The dead man was a terrorist; that much was obvious. If Cuban soldiers had eliminated him, regardless of their method, they'd have carted off the corpse and weapon for disposal. Cooper, on the other hand, had no time for such niceties.

The killing has begun, she thought, then checked herself. Matt Cooper's enemies—her enemies—had started this. They'd murdered hostages before he even came ashore, while she was waiting for him back at Bahia de Sangre. Anything that happened, until the last of them was killed or caged, was their fault.

And her next thought was as clear as crystal: She could leave, lay down the rifle and spare magazines, retrace her steps, reclaim her hidden scuba gear, and swim back to the point where she had left her car. She could obey Matt Cooper's orders, skip the worst of it entirely, and incur no guilt of any kind.

Except that which she heaped upon herself.

And if the tall American should die, so what? It was a risk he had assumed, coming to battle terrorists on soil where he was doubly foreign, as an Anglo and an agent of America's intelligence network.

Santos, already a traitor under Cuba's present laws, had no responsibility to join Cooper in combat. On the contrary, in fact, he had forbidden her to do so. Why, then, was she standing with a dead man's automatic rifle in her hands, prepared to follow Cooper and to sacrifice her life?

Because he shouldn't have to do the job alone.

Because, at least in her view, Cuba was responsible for the security of foreign visitors on Cuban soil. And if the government could not or would not do its job, perhaps she could redeem some measure of its tarnished honor.

Frightened, gripping her Kalashnikov so tightly that her knuckles ached, Maria Santos moved on toward the lighted tower block of the resort hotel.

9

Washington, D.C.

The Saudi ambassador's voice was like velvet in Nabi Ulmalhama's ear, but Ulmalhama knew that it disguised a fiery temper and a fist of steel.

"You've heard the latest news, I trust?"

"I have, Your Excellency," Ulmalhama said.

"At least one of the men at the resort in Cuba is a Saudi citizen. You've seen that on the television news?"

"I have," Ulmalhama repeated.

As if he had not spoken, the ambassador pressed on. "He's called Sarsour Ibn Tabari. Do we know him, Nabi?"

No, we don't, Ulmalhama thought. But I do.

Instead of voicing his most secret, guilty thoughts, he answered, "No, Your Excellency. I don't recognize the name. Perhaps, if you asked State Security—"

"I did exactly that," the ambassador said. "As it turns out, they know him very well indeed."

"In what regard?" Ulmalhama asked, feigning ignorance.

"He's well-known in extremist circles, active with the liberation fighters. With Hamas, al Qaeda, and most recently Allah's Warriors."

"I see."

"Not quite," the ambassador said, correcting him. "It

seems, also, that this Tabari's father is a friend of the royal family. He is involved with oil production—but, of course, who isn't?"

"Who, indeed, Your Excellency."

"He attended university in London with a cousin of the king. A cousin once removed, I think it is."

No worse than the bin Ladens, then, Ulmalhama thought.

"That doesn't seem so bad, Your Ex—"

"Compared to others we could name, eh? But this son, now, may become a great embarrassment for all of us. How long, in realistic terms, before the jackals of the media unearth the royal connection? Can you answer that, Nabi?"

"No, sir."

"Of course not. No one can. But I can tell you that the king is far from happy with this late turn of events. He is determined not to be humiliated in the public eye, forced to apologize for some pathetic cousin's friendship with the father of a madman."

"No. Why should he, sir?"

"Why should he? Let us ponder that," the ambassador said. "Perhaps, because of the Americans. Perhaps, because the insult to our Cuban friends—while they are weak and nearly insignificant—will also sting the Russians and Chinese."

"I understand, of course."

Was that a warning in the ambassador's voice, or was he simply sharing personal anxiety?

Ulmalhama reckoned that he knew the answer to that question. If careers—or lives—were riding on the line, he had no doubt that his superior would act with all dispatch to save himself. One word from the ambassador, and Ulmalhama could be on the next plane back to Riyadh and a grisly fate.

But why? How could the ambassador suspect, much less prove, Ulmalhama's involvement with Allah's Warriors?

A preemptive strike was called for, and he wasted no more time. "We should take steps to minimize the damage," Ulmalhama said.

"And what would you suggest?" the ambassador asked.

"You're worried that the media may find a link between this terrorist and his family," Ulmalhama said. "Why not eliminate the family, and thus remove the link?"

"As I explained, the father is—"

"A friend of the king's cousin, once removed," Ulmalhama said. "Yes, I understand, Your Excellency. But if someone of your stature should explain the problem to His Majesty, perhaps a distant cousin's feelings and a few small commoners the king has never met may be considered a small sacrifice to save the honor of the royal family."

For several moments, the ambassador said nothing. When he finally replied, his tone had taken on a brand-new measure of respect.

"You may be on to something, Nabi," he agreed. "If nothing else, the king should know his options in a situation of this kind."

"Yes, sir. I totally agree."

"As for the riffraff there, in Cuba…"

"I have no doubt they'll be dealt with in the harshest manner, sir."

"As they no doubt deserve. Good evening, Nabi."

"As you say, Your Excellency."

Ulmalhama knew that the ambassador would claim full credit for his plan, when it was finally suggested to the king. That suited Ulmalhama perfectly, since he had no desire to anger any member of the House of Saud, be it the king himself or some pathetic cousin born on the wrong side of the blanket.

The ambassador could take the credit and the risk. If the

plan blew up in his face and cast him out of favor, Nabi Ul-malhama would be next in line for a promotion in the Saudi diplomatic corps. The king would not name him ambassador.

Not yet.

Bahia Matanzas

BOLAN WAS STILL AT LEAST a thousand yards from the hotel when he heard voices whispering ahead of him, and slightly to his right. Since there was conversation going on, a muffled give and take, he knew at least two persons were involved.

More terrorists?

It made no sense to Bolan that the leader of an eight-man team would send three of his shooters out into the night, when there were still at least a thousand hostages to guard.

And more to be killed, the small voice in his head reminded him, in just about eight minutes.

Each successive execution would increase the tension between the captors and their prisoners. Sending one man outside to scout the grounds of the estate made sense, after the early military raid.

Sending two more out for a stroll was crazy.

Maybe these are crazy terrorists, he thought, then put that notion out of mind.

They might be vicious, homicidal predators, but nothing in that job description ranked them as insane, either within the medical or legal definitions of the term. Asim Ben Muhunnad had to know he needed every man and weapon he had left to guard the hostages inside the hotel tower and to carry out his threat of more executions every thirty minutes, if the White House failed to answer his demands.

So, who was out here chatting in the middle of the night?

Bolan had two clear choices. He could bypass the talkers,

whoever they were, and try to ignore them while hoping they'd return the favor.

Or, he could identify them. Neutralize them if it fell within the purview of his mission.

Not police, he thought, then faltered on the point of what to do with Cuban soldiers. They were hostiles in their own right, agents of a regime officially despised by Washington, but at the same time they were acting in a kind of law-enforcement role, opposing the same terrorists Bolan had been sent to find and liquidate.

He crept in closer, marveling at military men who'd never learned the basics of behavior in nocturnal ambush situations.

Soldiers on surveillance duty didn't smoke, chew gum or crack their knuckles. First and foremost, they did not engage in conversation where an enemy might overhear them and proceed as Bolan was, to seek out their position and eliminate the threat. Neither of these would graduate from boot camp, much less Special Forces training, if Mack Bolan was their judge.

This night, he might turn out to be their executioner.

Bolan had almost reached the source of the two voices when a subtle rustling in the ferns alerted him to danger on his left. He turned in that direction, bringing up his rifle, but he stopped short with the muzzle of an AK in his face.

"You want to meet my friends, gringo?" the man behind the rifle asked. "Okay, you get your chance."

"FIVE MINUTES," Muhunnad told the slender Palestinian beside him. "Then we kill ten more."

The Arab, Yasir Al Khalidha, shrugged as if to say that he had seen it all before. Ten corpses, more or less, meant nothing to him in the larger scheme of things.

Ten lives were nothing.

But a thousand! That would make them all immortal.

"You can choose, this time," said Muhunnad, as an experiment, to see if he could make the bland-faced Arab smile or grimace. Any sign of mental life at all.

Instead, the young man simply said, "Okay," thereby exhausting his supply of spoken English.

These young people today. What did they want, in Allah's name?

There was more muttering behind them, in the farthest corner of the hotel lobby. Muhunnad turned slowly toward the source of whispered conversation, picking out specific faces. When the time came—in four minutes—he might suggest that Khalidha pick some of his victims from that group, to silence their scheming.

He was about to mention it, when suddenly the compact phone in his pocket shuddered like a captive mouse trying to reach the light of day. Muhunnad stiffened as if he had touched a live electric wire.

Only one man still living knew the number of that telephone. There had been two, until Sohrab Caspari went down with the *Tropic Princess,* drowned in churning seawater and blood.

Muhunnad stepped away from Al Khalidha, seeking greater privacy before he took the phone from his pocket, opened it and said, "Hello?"

No salutation, as the stern, familiar voice asked, "How is your resolve?"

"Still strong," Muhunnad said.

"You've heard about the ship?"

"We have. It was…expected."

"Even so. How do you feel?"

Muhunnad knew the proper answer, had rehearsed it countless times. "Eager to strike for Allah and to join my comrades, sir."

"You are still keeping to the schedule, yes?"

The question made Muhunnad check his wristwatch. "Certainly. The next deadline falls in one minute, fifty seconds."

"Very good," the distant voice replied approvingly. I'll leave you to it, then. Our prayers of thanks are with you."

"Thank you, sir."

The line went dead, their brief connection severed somewhere out in space, cutting Muhunnad and his men adrift. There'd been no hope or plan for outside help, of course, no hint that he could possibly survive his mission. There was, thus, no basis for the fleeting but intense sensation of abandonment that Muhunnad experienced and just as swiftly put away.

Barely one minute left, until the pigs sacrificed ten more lives. It would not be Muhunnad's doing, even if he held the weapon and his finger pulled its trigger. He had given every chance to Washington and Tel Aviv, surely more time than they required to draw some cash from bloated banks and rubber-stamp the documents that would release his comrades from confinement.

What was so hard about that?

Instead of simply slaughtering his enemies, he had allowed them yet another chance to make amends for all the suffering they'd caused since 1948—indeed, since the beginning of recorded history. And even when the next ten sheep were dead, they would have another chance, and then another, and another after that.

More deadlines, until all the hostages were gone.

Unless the military tried to save them, first.

In which case, Muhunnad thought, he would give them all a big surprise.

THE VOICES TOOK Santos by surprise. She'd been so careful, creeping through the darkness, gauging every footstep, that the sound of voices whispering somewhere ahead of her was jarring, nearly as disturbing as an unexpected scream.

It didn't sound like Cooper talking, but she couldn't say for certain. Distance and the harsh distortion of a whisper foiled her effort to identify the voices.

There were two of them, at least. How else could they converse? She couldn't picture Cooper standing in the darkness, talking to himself. Which meant that he had either met someone, or else—

Santos checked herself. She didn't know if either voice she heard belonged to Cooper, and the only way to know was to continue on her present course, sneak up and view the gabbers for herself.

But was it worth the risk?

Suppose she'd stumbled on two Cuban soldiers, killing time on guard duty, with no idea that she or Matt Cooper were anywhere in the vicinity. Why risk her life or freedom to approach them in this way?

Simply because she had to know the truth and would not leave an active enemy behind her in the dark.

Santos crept forward, clutching her stolen rifle tightly, careful not to let her index finger stray inside the weapon's trigger guard. She had the safety off, a live round in the chamber, but she feared that any small sound in the bushes might prompt her to fire, without that precaution.

When she'd halved the distance to her destination, it became apparent to her that the men were speaking Spanish. Cooper claimed to speak some, but again, the muffled voices brought no image of his stern-but-handsome face to mind.

When she was ten or fifteen paces from the careless men, a third voice joined the conversation, still in Spanish. She could recognize the lilt of this, her native language, but the words themselves eluded her.

A few more cautious steps…

The third voice switched to English, saying, "One last time, gringo. Who are you, and what are you doing here?"

"My job," Bolan said.

"Your job in Cuba, gringo? Armed with these illegal weapons? Interfering with the military? We will have your name!"

"I doubt it," Bolan said, then lapsed back into silence.

One of the Cubans cursed him, as Santos scuttled forward, taking full advantage of their agitation and distraction. If she was correct, and there were only three soldiers with the man she knew as Matt Cooper, they might have a chance.

Not much of one, perhaps, but still a chance.

Santos saw them, finally, four men huddled together in a clearing. Three of them wore Cuban army uniforms, one sporting sergeant's chevrons on his sleeve, all three with automatic rifles aimed at Cooper.

Suddenly, Santos was behind them, saying, "Put your weapons down. Move slowly. Do not make me fire."

Two head swiveled to face her, while the third man kept his eyes and rifle fixed on Bolan. "Another one," the middle soldier said, sounding embarrassed. "Who are you?"

"I won't tell you again to put the rifles down," she said. She raised the AKSU to her shoulder. "Do it now!"

"She won't shoot through us," said the man still guarding Bolan. "She might hit her friend."

"I'll risk it," Santos said. "On the count of three. *One!*"

"She's bluffing," the holdout said.

"Two!"

Before she reached three, Bolan did something with his hands and snatched the stubborn soldier's rifle from him, whipping it around to slam the butt against his skull. The soldier dropped without another sound, leaving his two companions in a cross fire.

"Three," Santos said, and smiled as both men dropped their rifles, raising hands above their heads.

"You're not supposed to be here," Bolan said.

"You're welcome," she replied. "Now what about these two?"

"We can't just leave them," Bolan answered.

"You don't mean—"

He struck before she had a chance to tell him what he didn't mean, the wooden stock of his Kalashnikov making a hollow sound against the second soldier's skull and dropping him insensate to the ground.

The last soldier retreated, lurching toward Santos. It was easy, stepping up behind him, slashing with her rifle's butt toward the base of his skull. The metal stock rebounded from his thick neck muscles, staggering the soldier, but before he turned to face her, Bolan slammed his forehead with a solid blow that put him down.

"What happened," Bolan asked, "to waiting with the car?"

"I changed my mind," Santos said.

"Bad choice."

"I saved your life," she said indignantly.

Ignoring her, he checked his watch. "And now," he said, "we're out of time."

"OKAY, HE'S COMING over this way," James Foreman said. "Don't look at him, damn it! Just keep talking."

"About what?" the dealer from Vancouver asked.

"It doesn't matter what," Foreman replied, disgusted with the man. "Recite a nursery rhyme if you can't think of anything. Who cares?"

"Damn fool idea," the dealer grumbled. "Get us all killed, if you don't watch out."

"That's it! Just keep your voice down, so he can't hear what you're saying," Foreman ordered.

"Risk my life," the dealer groused, "and all for what? So you lot can play soldier, when you ought to be in rocking chairs? If this goes wrong—"

"You won't have anything to piss and moan about," Foreman broke into the lament. "The same as if we sit here, doing nothing. Either way, you'll still be dead."

"You don't know that. Stop acting like nobody else can have a thought but you, for Christ's sake! If I—"

"Closer," Foreman whispered, tracking the gunman with his peripheral vision while he leaned across the table toward the dealer, pretending to be engrossed by his words. "I'll tell you when he's close enough. Just wait."

"What were you in the service, anyway?" the dealer asked him. "Sergeant of the mess, I reckon, or the boogie-woogie bugle boy?"

"Another twenty feet," Foreman said, wondering if he could keep the dealer angry long enough to follow through on what they had agreed to moments earlier.

They needed more than simple whispered conversation, Foreman had decided, to draw one of their captors within striking range. An altercation should do nicely, just a bit of fisticuffs to bring the shooter rushing in and telling them to break it up.

Just bring him close enough to grab.

But it could still go wrong. If the approaching terrorist decided not to mix it up with angry hostages, he could stand back and shoot them from a distance, spray the whole damned table with his automatic rifle if he felt like it.

What would it cost the shooter?

He and his companions had already killed people in cold blood. Foreman was not conversant with the Cuban legal system, but he guessed that prison cells or firing squads were waiting for the kidnappers, no matter what they did from that point onward.

Still, he thought, if they had deadlines running and did not intend to slaughter everyone at once, right now, they had a stake in keeping order. Maybe that would be enough to bring the rifleman in close enough for him to reach.

"He's almost here," Foreman said. "Are you ready?"

"You bet your ass, I'm ready," the dealer snapped, lurching to his feet. "Get up, you prick, and take what's coming to you!"

Foreman smiled, rising, and said, "I thought you'd never ask."

SARSOUR IBN TABARI WONDERED if the men had lost their minds. Of course, he realized that they were under pressure, but to start a fistfight in the middle of a hostage situation was insane, beyond the pale of any normal thought process.

Cursing, he moved to separate them, felt Muhunnad watching as he closed the gap between himself and the combatants. Both were in their forties, at the very least, both taller than Tabari, but he did not fear them. They were frightened, possibly hysterical, and neither of them had a weapon.

If they had, he guessed they would have used the killing tools on each other first, before he could prevent them. It was funny, in a twisted sort of way, the aging tourists venting their anxiety on each other, when they really wished that they could kill Tabari and his comrades.

"Stop this now! Sit down!" Tabari snapped at them, advancing on the brawlers. Prodding with the muzzle of his weapon, he repeated, "I demand that you—"

The larger of the two combatants spun to face Tabari, grabbed the AK's muzzle, shoved it toward the ceiling, while his free hand formed a fist and slammed into Tabari's face.

Tabari clung with grim determination to his rifle, tried to call out for assistance, but his mouth was full of salty blood. Instead of crying out, he gargled. Hands were clutching at him from all sides, a kick sweeping his legs from under him. As he began to fall, Tabari squeezed the AK's trigger, rattling off a 3-round burst.

Around him, he heard screams. Both men and women were shouting, as the fists and feet slammed into him, bruising his hips and thighs, missing his groin by inches, opening his scalp to spill bright crimson on the polished lobby floor. The kick that broke his nose was stunning, nearly tipped him over into darkness.

From a distance, barely conscious now, Tabari felt the rifle twisted from his grasp.

More shots, and screams to match them. With his left eye swelling shut, the right filling with tears of pain, Tabari couldn't tell exactly what was happening. Someone was shooting, clearly, and they couldn't fail to find a target in the crowded lobby.

Pride and dizziness combined to stop him crying out in pain, as he was kicked and beaten. Someone slammed a metal chair across his thrashing legs. His left knee flared with agony.

More firing now, and hot brass fell around Tabari, one shell glancing off his bloody upturned face, another dropping down the open collar of his shirt. It stung, but seemed inconsequential with his other pains, the hammering that still continued as he bucked and shivered on the floor.

Tabari felt hands turning out his pockets, knew that one of them would find the folding knife he carried. If a bullet didn't find him first, that had to be the end. Why should they spare him? He would not have done as much for them.

Allah judged intent, not the result.

As something cold and razor-sharp plunged deep between his ribs, Sarsour Ibn Tabari hoped that was true.

"WE'RE TOO LATE," Maria Santos said, when they heard the sounds of gunfire from the hotel tower.

"For the next ten hostages," Bolan replied, "but not the rest."

The shooting should have stopped within a minute, maybe ninety seconds, but it didn't. Executing ten compliant victims was a butcher's task. The killers Bolan hunted wouldn't waste their ammunition on protracted firing unless—

"Something's wrong," Santos said. "There's too much shooting."

Suddenly, as if in answer to her words, the gunfire ceased.

"What is it?" she demanded.

"Trouble," the Executioner said. "We'll have to go and see what kind."

They were advancing, watching for more patrols around them, when Santos said, "The soldiers wouldn't try again. Would they? They lost too many men the first time. No, they couldn't."

Bolan hissed at her to still the futile and one-sided argument. "Be quiet, will you?"

"Sorry!"

They ran in silence after that, stopping once and seeking cover when a military helicopter thundered overhead to circle the hotel. Somehow, whether through spotters on the grounds or directional microphones, the Cuban military was aware of gunfire at the hotel.

"Will they move in now?" he asked Santos.

"I don't know. Perhaps, or—"

Two hundred yards ahead of them, the helicopter hovered near the hotel's entrance. Bolan supposed its passengers were angling for a look inside the lobby, trying to determine what was happening. A moment later, amplifiers mounted somewhere on the chopper blared commands from an authoritative voice speaking in Spanish.

At his side, Santos immediately translated. "It's a Captain

Esquivel," she said. "He wants to know who's shooting, and for what reason."

Twice the question was repeated from the hovering machine, before a man armed with a submachine gun stepped out of the lobby doorway, into Bolan's line of sight. His lips moved, but without a bullhorn, nothing he said was audible over the chopper's engine sounds.

Loudspeakers blared an order from the gunship.

"Captain Esquivel tells him to speak loudly," Santos said.

Bolan watched and waited while the hostage taker tried again, without success. It was a hopeless case, trying to speak with anyone inside the chopper from a hundred feet away, the airship's rotors thundering above.

At last, the whirlybird touched down outside the entrance. A man in uniform dismounted from the bubble cockpit and moved toward the gunman at the hotel entrance, keeping both arms raised at shoulder-height, displaying empty hands.

When they were ten or fifteen feet apart, the two men held a hasty conversation, each shaking his head in turn, before the soldier turned and jogged back to the helicopter. When he was aboard, it lifted off and roared back over Bolan's head, toward some point on the far perimeter.

"I wouldn't call that helpful," Bolan said.

Santos laughed, then caught herself. "Sorry," she said. "It's just…nothing."

"Ridiculous, you mean?"

She nodded and repeated, "Sorry."

"No, you're right," he said. "We still don't have a clue what's going on, and we *still* have to find a way inside."

A floor plan would have helped, but Bolan had been on the road—or, rather, in the air, then underwater—when the second team of terrorists had occupied Bahia Matanzas. There'd been no time or opportunity to obtain or transmit any plans.

"We obviously can't go in the front door," Bolan said.

"I know another way," Santos told him, smiling now.

"How's that?"

"This place is famous for its parties. I was once invited by a manager who hoped…well, never mind that. I was taken on a tour of the hotel. That night, I saw more than he did."

"Another way inside the tower," Bolan said, still skeptical.

"I'll show you, if you like," she said, and led the way without waiting to see if he would follow her.

10

Asim Ben Muhunnad and Yasir Al Khalidha crouched behind the hotel reservation desk, shielded from incoming fire by its bulwark of marble and masonry. Neither man dared raise his head to look around the lobby, where they still heard shuffling, scraping sounds—the latter made by sliding chair or table legs—and whimpered sounds of pain.

Muhunnad blamed Tabari for the whole damned mess. Bullets from Tabari's rifle were flying around his ears. The prisoners were furiously beating Tabari, and there had been a knife, blood slinging from its blade on the upstroke.

If Tabari was so foolish as to ruin everything they'd worked for all these months, then death was certainly the least that he deserved. Muhunnad wondered if such idiots were welcome in Paradise—and if, upon meeting Tabari in that glorious, idyllic place, Muhunnad would have the resolve to slap his face.

One problem at a time, he thought.

Right now, the problem was Muhunnad's hostages—or lack of same. Somehow, a group of them had plotted mutiny, even as Muhunnad stood and watched them, railing at them to be silent when they dared to whisper at their barren tables. Clearly, he had not been strict enough in that respect, should have considered shooting one or two for talking at the very start, but at least *he* had not supplied the hostages with a Kalashnikov.

Or, was it only one?

Muhunnad made a mental tally of his men. Tabari was eliminated, any weapons that he'd carried now in hostile hands. Khalidha was beside Muhunnad, seemingly unfazed by the bizarre turn of events. As for the rest, he had no memory of seeing Mahmood Tamwar when the shooting started, wondered if he'd run away or simply gone off to relieve himself.

Four others had been present in the lobby when Tabari lost his weapon to the prisoners: Cirrus Mehrzad, Bahram Parwana, Ishaq Uthman and Ghulam Yazid. They were all strangers to Muhunnad. He'd never met any of them prior to Camp X-Ray, but all had done their best for him so far. Whether the new radical departure from their plan had disconcerted them or not, their options were extremely limited.

They could desert him and surrender, if Muhunnad didn't kill them first, give up all hope of Paradise with a display of cowardice.

Or, they could stay and die like men.

The team leader had done his best to salvage what he could from the disaster. When the Cuban helicopter came and hovered outside the hotel, broadcasting a demand for an explanation of the shooting, Muhunnad had swallowed his fear of a shot in the back and went out to confer with the scowling officer. Muhunnad had reminded him of another deadline's passage without any positive response from Washington. More hostages had been dispatched, he said, and now the clock was running on *another* thirty-minute count.

The Cuban officer had left them as he came, still furious, but carrying Muhunnad's message. It would do no good, of course, in terms of any ransom payments, but at least Muhunnad thought he'd managed to deceive them on the way things stood inside the grand hotel.

How do they stand? Muhunnad asked himself.

And got no answer for his trouble.

He would have to risk a look around the lobby, drawing solace from the fact that no one had tried to kill him on his recent walk outside. Perhaps the hostages were saving ammunition for the moment when Muhunnad tried—as try he had to—to get Tabari's rifle back.

Or, had the armed ones somehow managed to escape?

That prospect brought Muhunnad close to panic. With the shooting and confusion, and afterward, the helicopter's visit and assorted other noise, he could have missed an elevator's chiming sound. Escaping captives could be literally anywhere in the hotel by now—or even on the grounds outside.

With only seven men at his disposal, Muhunnad had brought his captives to the lobby and corralled them there, keeping his soldiers close, instead of posting them around the long hotel perimeter. He'd trusted fear of cataclysmic retribution—hidden plastic charges, point-blank slaughter of the huddled innocents—to hold the Cuban soldiers at bay, in lieu of scattered lookouts.

Suddenly Muhunnad feared that he'd been wrong.

"Get up!" he told Khalidha, lurching to his feet in spite of fear. "We have much work to do!"

"ARE YOU SURE this is the right way?" Bolan asked.

"I'm sure," Santos said. "Come on."

They'd circled some three-quarters of the hotel's long perimeter, skirting some easy-looking entrances where gunmen might have lain in wait behind glass doors and windows offering a panoramic view of gardens, trees and swimming pools. The loading dock, by contrast, was a dark, deserted place.

It had the standard layout, parking bays for two large semi-trailers at a time, which would be backed in to dock while crews unloaded food, cleaning supplies, new furniture—whatever was required to keep a giant tourist operation up and running seven days a week, year-round. No trucks were present at the moment, though, and only one small light vied with the shadows pooled around the parking bays.

The doors were locked. Whether the terrorists or hotel staff had done it, Bolan neither knew nor cared. Santos was apologizing in a whisper, when he palmed a set of lock picks, chose two from the kit and got the door open in thirty seconds.

Locks were easy.

Hunting seven killers in a vast hotel was hard.

Bolan assumed the hostages had been collected in one place, where they could easily be watched. After the recent and erratic bursts of gunfire, though, he wasn't sure what they could expect or where it might be found.

They cleared the storeroom off the loading dock in nothing flat, near-empty as it was. Some wooden pallets and a small, new-looking forklift occupied the middle of the room, with half a dozen king-size mattresses stacked up against the northern wall. The exit door featured a window in its upper half, two layers of glass with wire mesh in between. Bolan peered out and checked the corridor beyond, as best he could.

"The lobby next," he whispered.

"Why?" Santos asked.

"It's where the shooting happened," Bolan answered. "Where the hostages should be, for visibility."

The terrorists wouldn't make it too hard on surveillance teams, or on themselves. They couldn't bluff for long. With murder deadlines falling every thirty minutes, and the gang's immediate response to queries from the Cuban chopper, Bolan knew they had to be somewhere near the lobby space, at least.

"That way," Santos said, pointing to their left along the corridor that served the storeroom and the loading dock. Another twenty paces, and concrete gave way to carpet underfoot. Beige paint gave way to floral wallpaper, and signs appeared, presenting them with choices.

Bolan began his hunt.

JAMES FOREMAN HUDDLED in a small utility room with his wife, the dealer from Vancouver and a male guest he didn't recognize. The stranger had to have followed them when they fled from the lobby, every hostage for himself, and joined them when they'd ducked into their hideaway.

Now, standing in the claustrophobic darkness—they had killed the lights as a precaution—Foreman wondered if they'd made a serious mistake. If they were trapped like rats, in fact.

"We should get out of here," the dealer muttered.

The dark disoriented Foreman, until he glanced down and saw a narrow strip of light beneath the door, intruding from the corridor outside.

Maybe he wouldn't hear the terrorists approaching, if they kept it quiet, but he ought to see them—or their shadows, anyway—before they opened fire.

He could start shooting, but the rub was that he wouldn't really know who he was shooting at, their captors or another clutch of fugitives like his, seeking a place to hide. And if it was the terrorists, what would he gain by firing blindly through the storeroom door?

He might hit someone accidentally, but killing more than one that way would take a miracle, not simple luck. And if he didn't get them all, disable them at least, then the survivors would return fire. Throw it back with everything they had.

And in the narrow confines of his hideaway, they couldn't really miss.

We could find someplace else, he thought.

No, they were stuck—at least for now, until the terrorists

stopped looking for escapees and went back to guarding their remaining prisoners.

Sweating in the glorified broom closet, Foreman clutched the rifle to his chest and settled in to wait.

Washington, D.C.

THE TELEPHONE CAUGHT Hal Brognola dozing at his desk. He was surprised, less by the jarring sound than by the fact that he had slept at all.

"Hello?"

"We've got something," Kurtzman informed him, without preamble.

"What's that?"

"A sat-phone call to the resort at Bahia Matanzas, from your own backyard," Kurtzman replied.

"Tell me you traced it, Bear."

"We traced it."

"And?"

"We're looking at one Nabi Ulmalhama, with a flat in Georgetown. He's a deputy of cultural affairs or some such at the Saudi embassy."

"Immunity?"

"Affirmative."

"Damn it!"

With diplomatic immunity, they couldn't even question the subject without his consent, much less sweat him in jail.

"E-mail me the particulars, will you?" the big Fed said.

"They should be waiting in your Inbox now."

"Okay. I'll give the file a look and call you back." He opened Kurtzman's dossier on Nabi Ulmalhama.

Twenty minutes later, he knew everything modern computers could dig up on Ulmalhama, from his birth in Riyadh to a privileged family, in 1963, through graduation with honors from Britain's Oxford University in 1985, with a bachelor's degree in political science. There was a two-year blind spot in the public record, after that, before Ulmalhama returned to Saudi Arabia in 1987, filling a slot that friends of his father had created for him in the nation's diplomatic service.

Ulmalhama's course from there, rising steadily but undramatically from a minor posting in Yemen to service at the Saudi embassy in Washington, was a textbook study of privilege and nepotism in action.

There was no information in the file concerning Ulmalhama's connection to Allah's Warriors. Brognola guessed he could find it somewhere, if he dedicated time, money and manpower to turning over rocks in every country Ulmalhama had ever visited—but what would be the point?

He knew that much of the covert funding for Islamic extremist groups came from Saudi Arabia. That ugly open secret haunted every member of the U.S. Diplomatic Corps who still had any vestige of a working conscience. But they followed orders, sucked it up and smiled when they were shaking hands with killers once removed.

In Ulmalhama's case, however, if Kurtzman was correct, support for terrorist activity had crossed the line from silent funding to active collaboration. The call from Ulmalhama's home to Bahia Matanzas—more specifically, to a sat phone carried by one of the terrorists there—elevated Ulmalhama's threat level to fire-engine red.

Of course, he was immune to legal punishment in the United States, couldn't receive a parking ticket, much less go to trial on charges of mass murder. Under any interpretation of international law, he was as free as a bird. The U.S. State Department could declare him persona non grata and boot him out of the country, but Brognola guessed they would need more evidence before offending a privileged son of oil-rich Saudi Arabia.

Right now, he thought that Ulmalhama had to be feeling good. Untouchable.

And he was almost right.

Bahia Matanzas

MARIA SANTOS HAD DECIDED that pursuing Cooper from the beach ranked as the worst idea she'd ever had. The second worst, she thought, was signing on to help the CIA. She could have led a normal life in civil service, found adventure on the weekends like her girlfriends, chasing alcohol and men.

But, no.

She'd wanted something different, to help her country and its people. Even to make sacrifices for the good.

Now that they'd penetrated the hotel, Santos feared the only sacrifice she made might be her life.

There was a smell of gunsmoke in the air as they approached the hotel lobby, following the signs posted in spacious corridors. They passed facilities installed for paying guests—a gym, computer room, a soundproof video arcade for children, conference rooms in varied sizes—all deserted now. Santos had the feeling of trespassing in a ghost town, and she didn't like it one damned bit.

The hotel's lobby, she recalled, was huge. It sprawled over an area the size of three or four normal homes, including a sunken lounge where musical combos played each evening from five to seven o'clock. There was a coffee bar, a separate station for the concierge, and space enough left over for a classic ballroom dance. She tried to picture it after the shooting, with the terrorists in charge, but couldn't hold the grisly image in her mind.

I'm shutting down, she worried. Losing it.

Except, she wasn't. It was something else, detachment from the violence she had witnessed and in which she had participated, bracing for worse things to come.

And it would certainly be worse if they encountered gunmen in the open corridor. She strained her ears for voices, footsteps, anything that might betray her enemies before they had a deadly face-to-face encounter. Even with the captured automatic rifle she felt unprepared, had only used it as a club so far, and she had needed Cooper's help with that.

It still wasn't too late for her to turn around, leave Cooper to proceed alone. She didn't think he'd mind, might even welcome her departure, but she'd come too far and risked too much to turn back.

My country, she repeated to herself. My fight.

And if it proved to be her last, at least she'd be remembered—as a traitor, by the government, and by the common folk as…what?

Nervous sweat welded her palms to the rifle she carried, making her worry that it would slip from her grasp if she had to use it. And even if not, could she hit anything? Anyone?

Why not? The men she stalked were terrorists, each one with countless murders to his credit, and they planned at least a thousand more before the night was over. Killing to stop a crime like that was not only permissible; she thought it might be mandatory.

But her hesitancy still remained.

She mouthed a prayer from childhood, whispered to her by her grandmother when no one else was listening. Castro's political machine had not suppressed the church as harshly as some other Communist regimes around the world, but many of the younger folk considered prayer a quaint and primitive pastime, akin to tossing spilled salt over the left shoulder and avoiding confrontations with black cats.

It couldn't hurt, Maria thought, and as the words took shape inside her head, she heard a muttering somewhere ahead of them. The sound was drawing closer by the moment, definitely emanating from a human.

She froze beside Matt Cooper, listening, and finally made out the words.

"Come here, little piggies. You can't hide from Cirrus. Come out little piggies and die."

CIRRUS MEHRZAD HAD BEEN relieved when Muhunnad chose him, along with Ghulam Yazid, to go to seek the hostages who had escaped during the battle in the hotel lobby. Mehrzad had cowered under cover during most of that frenzied engagement, firing only when he saw a number of the unarmed hostages escaping toward the elevators.

Muhunnad had been a fool to leave the elevators activated, when he could have trapped them easily on the ground floor, thereby preventing easy transport to the floors above. But he had overlooked that option, and roughly a quarter of the hostages had managed to escape—not only on the seven elevator cars, but via stairwells, ground-floor corridors and into service tunnels underground.

There were two hundred runners, more or less, before the rest were trapped and cowed into submission once again. That left eight hundred in the lobby, minus those who had been killed in the escape, and Muhunnad felt he could only spare two men to track the fugitives.

It stood to reason that Mehrzad and Yazid couldn't bring them back alive. That was not the assignment. Find them and punish them, Muhunnad said, no mention of returning them to join the others in the lobby.

Perfect.

It was something to amuse Mehrzad and let him place his own mark on the situation that was swiftly going sour. This way, when the soldiers came and killed him, he would know that he'd accomplished something for the movement.

For Allah.

The trick, now, was to find the sneaking infidels.

While there had been no time to memorize the hotel's floor plans in detail, Mehrzad was well acquainted with the basics. It had fourteen floors of guest rooms, plus the ground floor and the mezzanine devoted to shops, conference rooms and guest services. Below ground level, there was storage, maintenance and a garage for service vehicles.

So, make it eighteen floors in all. How many thousand square feet would that be? Mehrzad could not begin to guess, and didn't really care.

He planned to spend the rest of his life on this chore, and knew he likely wouldn't finish.

Such was destiny.

Yazid had gone up to the penthouse level straightaway, believing that the elevator hostages would ride as far as possible before they disembarked. It was a decent theory, but Mehrzad declined to follow him.

Instead, he chose the ground floor to begin his hunt, knowing that most of those who fled would find no place aboard the elevator cars, and some would shun the stairs as death traps, where a burst of automatic fire was bound to bring them down.

Those who remained on the ground floor would either seek an exit or go looking for a place to hide. Mehrzad believed that most, fearing the night outside, would go to ground.

But where?

He called to them, cajoling, hoping some would make it

easy on themselves. "Come here, little piggies," he warbled, almost in a child's voice. "You can't hide from Cirrus. Come out little piggies and die."

No one answered, so he checked each door in turn, cautious, remembering that one of the escapees had Tabari's automatic rifle, while another had his pistol and some kind of knife they'd used to mutilate Tabari's corpse. It was slow work, but he enjoyed it, savored the increasing thrill he felt as each deserted room meant he was getting closer to his prey.

Or was he?

Maybe those he sought had spilled into the darkness through a dozen different doors by now. Perhaps he was simply wasting time.

No matter, when he had so little left.

"Come here, piggies. Come out and die."

It couldn't be much longer, now. He would find someone, surely, and the killing could resume.

THE NEAREST COVER WAS a small computer room provided for the hotel's guests, five terminals lined up along a counter on one side, each with a plastic swivel chair. One monitor was decorated with an Out of Order sign, the other four displaying screen savers. A window in the door permitted passersby to peer inside. Lights off, the only place to hide was underneath the counter, pressed against the narrow room's east wall.

"He'll see us if he looks in through the window," Santos whispered.

"Fifty-fifty," Bolan estimated. "We should be all right if he's alone."

"I only heard once voice," she said.

That meant precisely nothing, Bolan realized. They'd have to wait and see how many shooters came to call, and do their level best to drop them.

Hiding in the dark room went against his grain, but Bolan didn't want to face hostiles without some kind of cover, while he had Santos in his shadow.

He steered Santos beneath the counter nearest to the door, trusting it to obscure her from the shooter's view. Bolan slid under, farther back, and shoved the nearest chairs out of his way. From where he lay, he had a fair shot at the door and could roll clear in nothing flat, to get a better line of fire.

From the outer hallway, muffled by insulation that was not quite soundproof, Bolan heard the hunter's mocking voice.

"Where are you, little piggies? Come out now and play."

Bolan twisted in his hidey-hole, angling the Steyr AUG to cover anyone who showed up in the doorway. Now it was a guessing game, deciding whether he was better off to shoot the first man visible, or wait until he knew if there was more than one outside.

An eye peered at him through the window in the door, then swiftly vanished. When the face came back a second time, it lingered, eyes roving around the dark computer room.

Their would-be killer couldn't see inside the room, Bolan surmised, because of lights behind him, glaring on the glass. To check the room and prove it safe, he'd have to step inside.

"I see you, little piggies," the shooter said.

Bolan waited, held his rifle steady at chest level, finger on the trigger, taking up its slack.

The shooter burst in on them, no one else behind him in the corridor. He heard Santos yelp and swung his rifle toward the spot where she was hidden, still not reaching for the light switch to improve his odds.

Bolan squeezed off a 3-round burst of 5.58 mm tumblers from a range of fifteen feet, punching his target backward, through the open doorway and across the hall. The dying man left smears of crimson on the wall as he slid down into a seated posture, then slumped over to his left and crumpled to the floor.

"Let's move!" Bolan said, rising even as he spoke and moving toward the door. "We don't have any time to waste."

11

The burst of gunfire startled Asim Ben Muhunnad. It had been short, precise and definitely not from a Kalashnikov or the Uzi carried by Ghulam Yazid.

Who, then?

That question set his mind in turmoil. Muhunnad could feel his pulse accelerate, each heartbeat thumping like a drum in his ears. It seemed so loud, he thought his men and all their captives huddled in the hotel lobby had to have heard it, but if so, they gave no sign.

Muhunnad paced the lobby, moving restlessly between the wall of glass and the sunken lounge area, then back again to the relative safety of the marble registration desk. At intervals, he glanced down toward his chest and legs, half expecting to find himself painted with red dots from enemy laser sights, but it was only his imagination. Then, each time, his harried mind snapped back to the real peril.

Someone was inside the hotel.

Muhunnad had calculated and accepted the risk of infiltration when he decided not to divide his small force and guard the hotel's extensive perimeter. He'd preferred to watch the hostages, be ready to smother them with gunfire at the first sign of intruders bent on rescue, and the plan had seemed a sound one at the time.

But it had blown up, literally, in his face.

Now he had hostages at large in the hotel, some of them armed, others perhaps escaped already from the building to make contact with the Cuban troops outside. His force of seven men was now reduced by three—one missing when he counted heads, two more dispatched to find and kill the runaways. And someone inside the hotel possessed an automatic weapon that had not come from his team or from the Cuban military.

The shots had come from somewhere relatively close at hand. The ground floor, certainly, and not so far away as to be muffled by a lot of intervening doors or walls. It seemed to Muhunnad that he could almost step around the nearest corner and behold his enemy.

But, no. Duty required him to stay where he was and supervise the execution of their grand scheme in accordance with its schedule.

Instead of going out to look himself, Muhunnad called to Yasir Al Khalidha, beckoned him and waited while the slender Palestinian came from the southwest corner of the lobby to join him.

"You've disabled all the elevators now?" Muhunnad asked.

"It's done," the younger man assured him. "No one going up or down unless I turn the key."

"You have it with you?"

"Yes." Khalidha patted the breast pocket of his baggy shirt to demonstrate.

"Give it to me," Muhunnad said, his open palm extended. "I have something else for you to do."

Khalidha handed him the small, round elevator key and asked, "What is it?"

"You heard the last few shots?" Muhunnad asked. It was a foolish question, but he had to start somewhere.

Khalidha nodded. "Yes. Not one of our weapons," he said, confirming Muhunnad's analysis.

"That's why we must identify the shooter and eliminate

him," Muhunnad declared. "I can spare only one man, and I judge you the best among them."

Muhunnad expected gratitude but got a kind of mocking smile instead. Khalidha half bowed, like a servant out of practice and replied, "Your wish is my command. Where should I start?"

"That way," Muhunnad answered, pointing to the east across the lobby. "Near the conference rooms, I think. It wasn't far. You may encounter them with no great difficulty."

"From your lips to Allah's ears," Khalidha said, and left Muhunnad standing by the check-in counter, moving off toward danger with an air of confidence Muhunnad envied.

Find the stranger in our midst and kill him, thought Muhunnad. Buy us time and peace before it is our turn to die.

THERE WAS NO DOUBT in Bolan's mind that everyone on the hotel's ground floor had heard his 3-round burst of fire from the computer room. The only question was whether Asim Ben Muhunnad would dispatch another man to hunt him down, or if the terrorist would keep his soldiers close, preparing for the final act of his suicidal drama.

Santos stalled him at the latest kill site long enough to strip their fallen enemy of magazines for his Kalashnikov, remembering the one already in his weapon. She looked almost comical with half a dozen clips tucked underneath her belt, a sexy pirate in her clinging swimsuit, but the danger still awaiting them smothered any urge to smile.

"Ready?" he asked.

"As I will ever be," she said.

"That's good enough. They know we're here, now," he informed her.

"Since the guns don't sound the same?"

"That's right." She wasn't just another pretty face. "They may come looking for us, or be ready with the hostages."

"What can we do, then?" she inquired.

"Our best," Bolan replied.

"Let's do it," she said grimly.

He led the way, from the computer room and bloody corpse outside, past other conference rooms and a gymnasium with glass walls.

Santos took the killing better than he'd thought she would, although so far she'd done none of her own. A part of Bolan hoped she would be spared that, but he knew the long odds were against her. They were either being stalked already, or they were moving toward a deadly ambush in the lobby. Either way, he guessed Santos wouldn't get away with simply watching from the sidelines.

They passed a small clothing shop, its window populated by headless mannequins with pale arms ending in smooth stumps, devoid of hands.

This is how the other half lives, Bolan thought. But they all die the same.

Santos followed Bolan closely, turning frequently to check the corridor behind them for approaching enemies. He caught her movements from the corner of his eye and reckoned she was doing all that could be done. The hotel was a warren built as if with ambushes in mind, and there was no way Bolan could protect them from all sides.

No way at all.

That was the price of hunting lethal predators. Sometimes—more times than he could count, in fact—the hunter was transformed into the prey.

Like now?

He wasn't sure, but Bolan knew one thing beyond a shadow of a doubt: he wasn't giving up. If he could swap his own life for a thousand hostages, he'd reckon it a decent trade.

"IS THAT MORE SHOOTING?" the dealer from Vancouver asked.

"No," Foreman answered. "They're just setting off fire-works to celebrate the holiday."

"What holiday?"

Foreman ignored him, then impulsively declared, "I'm getting out of here. Come on, Irene."

"Come where?" his wife demanded from the darkness. "That was shooting and you know it. Where in hell are we supposed to go, Jimmy?"

"We'll be safer on the move than waiting here."

"Since when?" the stranger challenged. "First, you said we be safer in here."

"I changed my mind, goddamn it! Listen, you don't have to come along, all right? You want to wait here, fine. Irene and I—"

"Not me," she interrupted him. "I'm staying put."

"I know you're scared," he said. "It's natural. We simply don't have time to argue now."

"Who's arguing?" her waspish voice came back. "You want to walk out in the middle of a shooting gallery. I'll take my chances here."

"You don't know what you're saying," Foreman challenged.

"Wrong," Irene replied. "You don't know what you're doing, Jimmy. It's been years since you were in the service, and you never left the country, much less went to war. This isn't just another weekend paintball game, you know!"

He found the light switch, flicked it on and watched the others squint under the sudden glare. The stranger looked away from Foreman and his gun. The dealer from Vancouver met his eyes but wisely kept his mouth shut.

Irene, half his height and weight, stood firm.

"I know it's not a bloody game," Foreman said, taking care

to keep eye contact, one thing that she always seemed to value. "But if we stay here—"

"The way you said we should, five minutes earlier?"

"I said I've changed my mind, damn it!"

"Well, I have not. I will not go out there."

"Irene—"

"Keep your voice down!"

Chastened, whispering, he told her, "I was wrong, okay? Does it please you to hear me say it?"

"Nothing in this goddamned situation pleases me."

"I'm going out to look for help. If you insist on staying here—"

"That's what I said."

Foreman could feel his stomach twisting into knots. "All right, then. I'll be back as soon as possible."

"You'd really go and leave me here?"

"Somebody has to do it."

Blushing with embarrassment, he turned and reached out for the doorknob. Irene's voice was like a whiplash, cutting into him.

"Can you kill the lights, at least, before you go?"

He slapped the switch, let darkness hide his flush of shame, then found the knob again and turned it, peering out into the corridor. The open door let Foreman scan the hallway to his left, while blocking any view off to his right.

He stepped across the threshold, turned and softly shut the door behind him. They'd be fine, in there, until he found a group of soldiers or police and told them what had happened, how he'd led a mutiny against the terrorists and given others time to run. He'd lead the real professionals back to the place where Irene and the others waited, then stand down and let them do the rest.

Foreman could almost see his photo in the newspapers, imagined being interviewed and heaped with praise on television. Maybe he could sell the story to a film production company, even earn something extra as a technical adviser. Write a book, or have some ghostwriter produce one for him, then sit back and watch the royalties pour in.

Heroic deeds were currency. Irene would understand that, in the end.

Smiling, James Foreman turned and made his way along the corridor, eastbound. At the next corner, he paused briefly, listened, then advanced.

A swarthy gunman blocked his path.

MARIA SANTOS FLINCHED as yet another burst of gunfire echoed through the deathly still hotel. Those rounds, she knew, were fired from a Kalashnikov. Its rattling sound was unmistakable.

Not shooting us, at least, she thought, and instantly felt guilty.

Bolan paused in front of her, head cocked and listening, then cautiously resumed his course along the hallway. On their left, a door was labeled SPA in gold gilt letters. The windows to that room were mirrored glass.

Another shop was situated on her right, this one devoted to accessories including jewelry, expensive wristwatches, and handbags wildly overpriced. No Cuban other than an aging party leader could afford such things—but, then again, how many Cubans even knew the shop existed? If she traveled far and wide throughout the country, how many of those she questioned would know anything at all about Bahia Matanzas?

It makes no difference, she told herself. These people must be stopped.

Mentally she had known she'd have to kill them, was prepared to do it since she'd decided to trail Cooper from the beach. Unfortunately, as she'd learned since stumbling on the first corpse of the night and stealing the dead man's rifle, there was a world of difference between mentally preparing and doing the actual deed.

Matt Cooper, clearly, had been down this bloody road before. Not once, but many times.

She wondered how it felt to kill so casually—or was that a misperception of the man? Was he, perhaps, roiling with emotion inside, and simply adept at concealing it? Did he agonize over each man he killed? Lose sleep at night, remembering their vacant, lifeless faces?

Santos couldn't read his mind, but she imagined that he had some kind of life beyond his weapons and the killing. That he stepped back, somehow closed his mind to it, and managed to enjoy himself sometimes.

More to the point, if *he* could do it, so could she.

But first, she had to live through the experience.

Her blood was up. She understood that saying now, had always thought that it referred to men alone, when they were hunting animals or women, chasing thrills in a casino or a tavern. Now, she understood, it simply meant a stark awareness of the world around her, and the knowledge that it could be snatched away from her—or she from it—at any time.

How long until they reached the lobby and were forced to fight a desperate battle for their lives, the lives of countless strangers? She had walked these carpets once before, but now felt strangely lost, fearing she might have misled Cooper when it mattered most. But how could that be, when they followed all the posted signs?

You're getting paranoid, she told herself.

Yet another burst of gunfire rattled through the vast ground floor of the hotel. The big American stopped dead in front of her. She almost trod on his heels. She spun, but found no gunmen creeping up behind her.

Still, the sound was closer now.

"This way," Bolan said, before veering off their posted course, along another hallway leading south.

They would miss the lobby this way, or at least take more time reaching it, but she did not challenge his choice. The warrior seemed to know what he was doing.

Or, at least, she hoped so.

If his choice was wrong, it might well cost their lives.

YASIR AL KHALIDHA STOOD over the man he had killed, examining the pale, pain-twisted face for hint of the man's last thoughts. It proved a futile exercise, leaving Khalidha with the most important questions still unanswered.

Where had this one come from?

And were others close at hand?

Before continuing along his way, Khalidha knelt and pulled the magazine from the dead man's rifle, working the slide to eject its last round from the chamber. It was Tabari's rifle, taken when the hostages had killed him, but Khalidha didn't need a second weapon. By unloading it, he made it useless to the others unless someone tried to use it as a club.

Where did he come from?

That was easy—or, the first part of it, anyway. The man had walked around the nearest corner, coming from an east-west corridor that ran past conference rooms and offices. From there…

Khalidha hesitated at the corner, then felt foolish and stepped boldly around it, his AKSU leveled from the hip. The empty hallway sneered at him for his precautions.

Counting closed and silent doors, Khalidha found four on his right, five on his left, before he reached the next junction of corridors.

Should he try all of them?

Why not?

The first two doors were locked. He stood and rattled each in turn, then listened closely for a sound that might betray his quarry, hiding in the dark. When no sound issued from those rooms, he moved on to the third and tried its door.

The knob turned at his touch.

Khalidha shoved his way inside, crouching, sweeping the dark room with his AKSU rifle. No one squealed or rushed out to attack him, so he fumbled for the light switch and eventually found it. The fluorescent fixtures overhead revealed a room equipped for business meetings, a long table in the middle, lined with half a dozen chairs on either side.

The chairs were vacant. He found no one hiding underneath the table.

Muttering a curse, Khalidha turned and crossed the hallway in a rush, trying an unmarked door directly opposite the conference room. It also opened readily, but outward this time, forcing him to take a short step backward from the threshold.

"No!" a woman's voice cried out to him, from what appeared to be a storage room of sorts. "Please, don't!"

Khalidha saw them now, the woman and two men huddled together.

"Out!" he snapped at them. "Outside, here!"

They obeyed, Khalidha backing off to give them room as they emerged. He checked their hands, empty, no weapons visible. That left Tabari's pistol and a knife still unaccounted for, but if these three were hiding them, he'd find out soon enough.

"You're brave, yes?" As he spoke, Khalidha let them see his most engaging smile. "You make escape from evil terrorists and kill one, eh?"

"Whoa there, my friend," the larger of the two men said. "We haven't killed anybody."

"No? You should be proud of fighting," Khalidha said. "Real men fight. You want to fight me now?"

"No, sir," the first man said. The others were content to shake their heads, emphatic negatives.

"Okay," Khalidha said, shrugging. "I let you go. Bye-bye."

They gaped at him, then flicked suspicious glances back and forth between themselves. Another moment passed before Khalidha said, "You deaf? I say to you, go free. Run far. Go now!"

A gesture with his rifle on the last two syllables put them in motion, turning, almost bumping into one another as they ran.

Khalidha smiled and brought the rifle to his shoulder, holding down its trigger as he swept the blazing muzzle left to right, then back again.

"Run free," he told the crumpled dead, and barely heard his own voice, for the ringing in his ears.

MUHUNNAD FLINCHED every time the guns went off, hating himself for the involuntary movement, hoping no one else had seen it. Weakness now, in any form, could utterly destroy him and the plan of which he was a crucial part.

At least, this time, he recognized the sound of a Kalashnikov—but what did that mean, when the fugitives had made off with Tabari's, and the Cuban army used the same rifles?

Nothing.

Two bursts of fire, the second longer, separated by perhaps two minutes. Was that gap significant? Did it portend a victory for his men, or defeat?

Muhunnad didn't know, but he was sure he would send no more of his remaining soldiers to traipse the hotel corridors, looking for trouble, when they had enough in front of them to last the brief remainder of their lives.

If there were soldiers creeping toward them, or if some of the escapees were returning for their friends, they'd find Muhunnad and his men waiting to face them in the lobby.

After they had slaughtered the remaining hostages.

Muhunnad checked his wristwatch, noting that another fourteen minutes still remained before his next deadline for executing ten more prisoners. He reckoned they should go ahead with it, unless the Cubans tried to stage a rescue first.

Once rules had been established, they should be observed. Without them, there was only anarchy.

The Cubans had surprised him, waiting this long, but he guessed their failure early on had tempered their enthusiasm for heroic measures. They'd been bloodied once already, and were not prepared to bleed again for strangers, much less a gaggle of filthy-rich capitalists.

No problem there, since no one in Allah's Warriors—least of all him—had thought they would succeed with their demands. It was a calculated game they played, with deadly consequences.

And the game was winding down.

One way to throw his enemies off balance, Muhunnad supposed, would be to execute the next ten hostages ahead of schedule. It appealed to him, both as a piece of strategy and as revenge for their rebellion, but Muhunnad finally decided to observe the schedule issued with his first demands.

If he played by the rules, the White House could not claim that it was sandbagged or betrayed. The next ten deaths, and each new round of executions after that, would be a fair slap in the face for Washington.

And that, in fact, was what Muhunnad's game was all about.

He'd come a long way from his homeland, volunteering to give up the last years of his life to make a point—scrawl it in blood across a world of television screens and newspapers, in fact. In death, Muhunnad knew he would become another nail in America's coffin, one more germ infesting the decadent giant's bloodstream.

There were worse ways to die than serving the cause and God. For the first time since the escape, Muhunnad smiled.

BOLAN WAS HUNTING NOW, not simply moving toward a stationary target. Somewhere in the winding corridors ahead, within a hundred yards, a killer prowled.

Bolan surmised that the most recent bursts of AK fire, separated by roughly two minutes, had come from a terrorist's weapon. If there were Cuban soldiers inside the hotel, they would be pressing an attack on Muhunnad's guerrillas in the lobby. And since no attack was under way, that told him any mopping up around the place could only be some effort by his enemies.

It was a lethal effort he was duty bound to interrupt.

"Where are we going?" Santos whispered from behind him.

Bolan wagged a cautionary finger in her general direction, and she didn't ask again.

After the latest bursts of shots, he'd heard a pair of mismatched women's screams from the direction of the lobby. Those sounds helped confirm for the Executioner that the shots had come from somewhere else. He had a fix on their direction now, but he wasn't sure if he could trust the large hotel's acoustics. Likewise, he assumed that the shooter—his target—would be on the move.

He thought they had to be getting close, but Bolan's unknown target didn't offer any help this time. He wasn't calling out to little piggies, wasn't talking to himself or making any other noise that would help to pinpoint his location. The oppressive silence following the last two bursts of autofire made Bolan hesitate at every turn and corner, bracing for a hail of hostile lead each time he made a move.

And still, nothing.

They'd covered forty yards or so of look-alike hallways,

passing expensive shops and enigmatic numbered doors, when Bolan thought he saw a shadow stretching toward him on the wall directly opposite, around a gentle curve. He froze and hit a crouch, Santos mimicking his every move.

The gunman saw Bolan immediately, reeling backward even as he fired a short burst from the hip, his bullets knocking divots from the wall and ceiling. The Executioner instantly returned fire, thought he might've winged the guy, but more AK fire spoiled his follow-through.

A backward glance showed him Santos, squatting on her haunches, back against the wall. Her wide eyes didn't have the panicked look he'd seen in some novice combatants, but she clearly wasn't happy with their situation, either.

Bolan palmed a stun grenade.

Frag would've been his preference, but he couldn't risk it with the hostages still unaccounted for. He yanked the flash-bang's pin and put his weight behind the pitch, a lob that bounced his canister off the opposite wall and sent it wobbling around the blind curve in the hallway.

"Ears," he warned Santos, clapping hasty hands over his own before the echo of the blast assaulted them. The flash wasn't a problem, not directly visible from where they'd hunkered down, and Bolan kept his eyes open, although diverted from ground zero.

With the thunder still reverberating, he rose and scuttled cautiously around the corner, Santos trailing him. He found the scruffy shooter kneeling, slumped against a wall, using his AKSU rifle as a cane to brace himself upright.

The gunman blinked at Bolan, recognized his last mistake and tried to bring up the Kalashnikov, but he was out of time. A 3-round burst from Bolan's weapon tattooed the man's chest and dumped him over backward, legs folded beneath his supine body.

"Want another rifle?" Bolan asked Santos.

"No," she answered, "but I'll take the magazines."

Good move, he thought, watching as she stripped the corpse of three more magazines. Two fit beneath her belt, which left a spare until she stuffed it down inside the neckline of her bathing suit.

The Executioner resumed his hunt.

12

Ghulam Yazid was running out of steam. He had already searched the hotel's penthouse, scowling in envy at the decadence around him, and discovered no one hiding there. On the eleventh floor, he'd shot a solitary hostage, which improved his temper but did nothing for his wind.

Because Muhunnad had finally trapped all elevators on the ground-floor level, Yazid had to use the stairs. Granted, the way was all downhill, after he started at the tower's summit, but a sense of urgency still made him scurry in the stairwell, bursting out to rush along each hallway, racing door to door. His master key card, furnished by the hotel's cringing manager, granted Yazid access to every room he passed, but so far, finishing on ten, he had found no one else to kill.

Dragging and disappointed, he was on the second flight of stairs descending from the tenth floor to the ninth, when gunfire and a grenade blast echoed through the stairwell from below.

Ground floor, he thought, and when Yazid could not explain his certainty with any bit of evidence, he thought again, Where else?

The shooting could mean anything—another deadline passing, more unrest among the hostages—but the explosion was a different matter altogether. Muhunnad would not use hand grenades except in dire emergency. Another raid by Cuban troops, perhaps.

Yazid stood frozen on the stairs for a moment, conjuring an image of his death. He was determined that he would not go back to Guantanamo, nor was he ready for a life term in a stinking Cuban prison, fighting rats and roaches for his daily crust of bread. Having escaped from hell on Earth already, he would not return as long as he had strength enough to make a fist or pull a trigger.

If soldiers were attacking, Yazid needed to rejoin his comrades in the hotel lobby. If some other crisis had arisen, which his mind could not imagine at the moment, they might also need his help.

Yazid's dilemma was whether to follow orders and keep searching for the runaways, or use his own initiative and go downstairs.

He puzzled over it for thirty seconds more, and then decided he could not afford to miss the final showdown, if in fact it had begun. Cursing the hostages who might escape him, Yazid began to jog downstairs, his raspy breath and footsteps loud inside the stairwell.

Passing the sixth floor, he paused to rest and readjust the shoulder strap of his Uzi submachine gun. While slumped against the landing's rail, he considered that he might defeat his purpose with a headlong rush downstairs. What if his enemies were waiting for him, heard him coming like a wildman, making so much noise, and ambushed him before he had a chance to fire a shot?

All wasted, then, his zeal and dedication to the cause.

More caution, he decided, was the wiser course. When he moved out again, Yazid went slower, planting each step coolly and deliberately. He held the Uzi ready, breathing through his nose and listening for any sound of footsteps on the stairs below him.

He would not allow the Cuban thugs or anybody else to

take him by surprise. Yazid knew that his hours were numbered, but he wouldn't simply throw his life away, as if it had no value. He could still fight, take as many adversaries with him as he had rounds in the submachine gun's magazine.

He would arrive in Paradise a hero, ready to accept his just reward.

And if that meant a bit of suffering before the end, at least he knew that there would be blood and pain enough to go around.

MUHUNNAD CLUTCHED his assault rifle to keep his hands from visibly trembling. He felt his nerves unraveling and wondered how much longer it would be, before he lost control.

Not only gunfire in the corridors around him, now, but hand grenades. None of the men he'd sent to search for fleeing hostages carried grenades, which reaffirmed his sense that they were no longer alone in the hotel.

Soldiers?

Muhunnad had considered the idea and instantly rejected it. If the Cubans had worked up the nerve for another attack, they would swarming through the lobby now, instead of playing cat-and-mouse in other parts of the ground floor. Why waste grenades on empty rooms, when they could blast Muhunnad and his men?

A war of nerves, perhaps, he thought, but then dismissed that notion, too. The Cubans were not known for subtlety. Their notion of psychological warfare was to kill a target's wife and children, leave the bodies in his home and frame him for the crime.

No, Muhunnad did not believe the soldiers would play hide-and-seek, when they already knew exactly where his men were, with their prisoners.

Most of the prisoners, at least.

One of the hostages?

Again, in made no sense. Where would the fugitives acquire grenades or automatic weapons in a caliber distinct and separate from any carried by Muhunnad's raiders? It seemed impossible.

The Cubans could have different weapons, something with a lighter caliber than their standard-issue Kalashnikovs, but that brought Muhunnad back full-circle to his original objections.

No. It had to be someone else.

He hated the uncertainty.

The hostages were calming down at last, after the latest gunfire and explosion. Shouting at them when they were in such a state only produced more sobbing from the women, angry glowers from the men. Muhunnad did not care what they might think of him, since he intended to kill all of them in any case, but with the memory of one rebellion fresh in mind—Tabari's corpse still leaking in its cast-off place behind the registration desk—he shied away from risking yet another upheaval.

He was reduced to three men in the lobby now, counting himself, while seven had been insufficient to prevent the first escape. It seemed impossible to Muhunnad that no one in the mass of hostages had done the same arithmetic.

Only a fool rattled a basket filled with vipers, if there was a chance they could escape and bite him.

Muhunnad had positioned his remaining guards—Bahram Parwana and Ishaq Uthman—so that their guns and his comprised a three-way cross fire, if the hostages tried anything at all. He had instructed both, and told the prisoners as well, that there would be no further warnings. Anyone who stood up, spoke, or otherwise created a disturbance would be shot and left precisely where he fell.

That left Muhunnad with the problem of his next approaching deadline for mass execution. He had seven minutes left before he had to kill ten more hostages, in order to maintain his credibility.

But did it matter?

Was the risk of calling ten out from the ranks too great, under the present circumstances? Should he simply shoot ten where they sat? And what would the remaining hundreds do, in that case?

Maybe he should scrap the program altogether, choose an arbitrary time—ten minutes or an hour, anything that suited him—and kill them all, without another threat to the authorities who would not yield, in any case.

Before he did that, though, Muhunnad wanted reinforcements. He would use his cell phone, call Mehrzad, Tamwar, Khalidha and Yazid back to the lobby, where their guns were badly needed now.

If they are still alive, Muhunnad thought, and hesitated, with the telephone in hand.

He was afraid to call and get no answer, more afraid to hear a voice he did not recognize come on the line to tell him what his heart of hearts already knew—that death was coming for him, and it wouldn't be put off.

"YOU RECOGNIZED HIM, yes?" Santos asked, her voice a whisper. "All three, maybe?"

"Two of them," Bolan answered, pausing at a corner before moving onward. "Faces from a file. Escapees from Guantanamo."

He didn't burden her with names of those he'd killed so far: Mahmood Tamwar, Cirrus Mehrzad. The third he hadn't recognized, assuming that he'd been a member of the Gitmo raiding party led by Muhunnad.

"How many left?" Santos asked, surprising him with the direction of her question.

"Should be four," he said, "based on the size of chopper they requested for their getaway."

"That's not so bad," she said. And when he glanced at her, one eyebrow raised, she smiled and said, "I'll just be quiet, now."

Perfect.

Unless they met more opposition on the way, or heard more shooting from another corner of the floor they occupied, Bolan saw no reason why they should not go straight on to the hotel lobby and attempt to liberate the hostages. They were about to miss another deadline, as it was, and Bolan feared that his use of a stun grenade against his last opponent might advance Muhunnad's schedule.

They cleared another section of the hallway—more shops, offices and guest facilities abandoned in the midst of crisis—and he paused to check the intersection of right-angle corridors before proceeding. In the midst of it, he felt Santos tugging lightly on his sleeve, and turned to face her.

"I apologize," she whispered, leaning closer to him, "but there's something more that I must ask."

"Make it quick," Bolan said.

Nodding, she continued, "When we reach the lobby, what are we to do?"

It was a valid question, which he couldn't answer without having seen the layout, noting how the gunners and their captives were arranged. There were too many hypotheticals involved for Bolan to dictate their strategy without at least a quick glimpse of the killing ground.

And killing was the only given. He could not expect the terrorists to drop their weapons and surrender. It defied their personalities, their culture, their religious upbringing.

Muhunnad and his refugees from Camp X-Ray had come here for a reason, and it smelled like human sacrifice. Bolan didn't believe that they were really after money, really hoping for release of prisoners they couldn't even name in their demands. It all felt like a setup to the Executioner, stage dressing for mass murder, as had happened with the *Tropic Princess* earlier.

In Bolan's mind, the Bahia Matanzas hostages were dead if he did nothing, so it didn't really matter what he tried, or how it played out in the end. If he saved five or ten out of a thousand, that was five or ten who would have died without his intervention.

Bolan had come prepared to kill for strangers, and to die for them if necessary. Those he tried to help would never know his name or have a chance to thank him; some might never even glimpse his face.

And what about Maria Santos?

Bolan hadn't thought it through, but she was also skating on the thinnest of thin ice. A candidate for prison, torture and perhaps a firing squad, if her connection to the CIA should be revealed. It had been her choice, following him from the beach—and she had definitely helped him with the soldiers—but he still regretted her decision to become involved.

Saving her from the Fidelistas, from herself, might be more difficult than rescuing the hostages. In fact, Bolan wasn't convinced it could be done.

His exit strategy from the resort had been a one-man plan, Santos waiting with her car at Bahia de Sangre when he got there, but that plan was blown. They'd have to play the rest by ear, if they survived the next few minutes.

Pushing defeatist thoughts away, Bolan turned left and pressed on toward the lobby where the hostages were held.

GHULAM YAZID WAS panting by the time he reached the second floor. It seemed ridiculous to stop and rest when he was so close to his goal, but he felt dizzy from the headlong rush downstairs, worried that it would spoil his aim or his reaction time, if he was suddenly confronted with an enemy.

The Uzi seemed to weigh much more than its nine-point-whatever pounds with a full magazine. Yazid could barely hold it in his sweat-slick hands, until he took turns wiping one palm, then the other, on his denim pants. That helped, but then he had to wipe the gun itself, using his shirttail, nearly fumbling it before he finished.

Guilt drove him down the last two flights of stairs before he felt ready, but he couldn't bear the thought of stalling any longer. Muhunnad and his companions needed all the help that they could get.

But how could he, Ghulam Yazid, best help them?

Rushing to the hotel lobby was one option, but he reckoned Muhunnad would want to know why he was back so soon, and why he brought no runaways with him. Yazid could always tell the truth, say that the sound of gunfire and grenades had brought him back to fight beside his fellow warriors—but would that be good enough?

He wasn't sure.

Muhunnad was a hard man to please. It might be better, in the long run, if Yazid sought out the enemies who'd infiltrated the hotel and tried to kill or capture them. It might spell death for him, but what else had he come to find at Bahia Matanzas?

Death had been anticipated—and he found it preferable to the snide abuse his chief would heap upon him for ignoring orders.

Find the enemy. Confront them. Kill them.

Certainly. But how?

The answer, Yazid thought, was obvious. His enemies would go for Muhunnad, his warriors and the hostages. Yazid needed only to scout the various approaches to the lobby and be waiting at the right one when they came.

He would keep moving, searching, until he made contact with his prey. Then, he would fall upon them with righteous wrath and kill as many as he could before they cut him down. Perhaps, with luck, he might even emerge victorious. A hero.

Hesitating with his left hand on the doorknob of the first-floor access door, Yazid knew that his victory scenario was totally implausible. He wasn't there to win, but rather to complete a sacrifice dictated by the leaders of Allah's Warriors.

For the cause.

And there was no time like the present to begin.

He turned the knob, pushed through the door and moved along an empty hallway, stalking human prey.

WITH EVERY STEP SHE TOOK, Maria Santos fought an urge to turn and run. Each time she checked the corridor behind her for approaching enemies and found it empty, she was gripped by a desire to flee and leave Matt Cooper on his own.

The worst part was that Cooper likely wouldn't care.

He was a solitary warrior, did things his own way, and clearly had no patience for an amateur who tagged along without an invitation.

Three men were dead now, since she'd joined him, and three Cuban soldiers beaten senseless on the grounds outside. She offered up a silent prayer that none of them had seen her face clearly enough to spot her later, in a lineup or a crowd.

Prison would be the very least she could expect for an assault on soldiers in performance of their duties. The security police would want to know why she was present in the first place, much less armed and interfering in a siege with Muslim terrorists. They would interrogate her privately until she gave them answers they were willing to believe. No doubt, they would reveal her CIA connection in short order, once the pain began.

Then, what?

A cage for life, with cruel men to guard her and torment her for their own amusement?

Or a firing squad?

She worried less about herself than the remainder of her family, knowing the way in which the Fidelistas punished crimes against the state by making an example of spouses, parents, siblings, aunts and uncles.

At the very least, her kinfolk would be ridiculed, humiliated, by their neighbors, their employers, coworkers, the merchants whom they dealt with on a daily basis. If the state desired it, they could also be imprisoned—even executed— as alleged conspirators.

There were two ways to spare her family that risk, that shame. She could escape, leaving behind no trace of her involvement in the raid, or she could die in such a manner that her corpse was not identified.

She could seize one of Cooper's hand grenades, perhaps, and use it on herself if they were cornered helplessly. Make sure she grabbed the right one, too—an antipersonnel grenade, with shrapnel to shred her, instead of the loud but nonlethal canisters he used to stun his enemies.

Courage was all she needed when the moment came.

But would she have enough?

A door opened behind her, suddenly. She spun and dropped into a crouch, her index finger tightening around the AKSU's trigger. She felt Cooper at her side, aiming his rifle in the same direction as a frightened-looking man with empty hands emerged from a darkened office.

"Don't shoot!" the stranger blurted out.

"Who are you?" Cooper asked him.

"Nobody. I mean, Joe Danforth…just a guest at the hotel. Please don't—"

"A hostage?" Cooper interrupted.

"Well…I was. We were. Some of us got away."

"How many?"

"I'm not sure."

"The shooting," Santos said.

To the trembling man, the warrior said, "Get back in there and lock the door. Stay out of sight. You're not safe wandering the halls."

"Okay," Danforth said, "but are you—"

"Go *now!*"

Bobbing his head, the hostage ducked back out of sight and closed the door. Santos heard its lock engage.

"More trouble," she said.

"They could turn up anywhere," Bolan acknowledged. "Wandering across the line of fire."

Santos was embarrassed that she'd been thinking first about herself, seeing the hope for her survival and escape slip through her fingers.

If the hostages—or some of them, at any rate—were running free through the hotel, it was only a matter of time until some got outside. When that happened, the troops surrounding Bahia Matanzas would have no excuse for hanging back.

And when they finally attacked, all hope was lost.

Cooper was good, might even find a way to kill the four remaining terrorists without losing too many hostages, but she could not believe that he'd outwit the Cuban army. Thinking only of the numbers, he was surely doomed.

And so was she.

YAZID HEARD MUFFLED voices, followed by the closing of a door. The voices spoke in English, which he recognized but barely understood. Distance and unfamiliarity conspired to strip all meaning from the words.

But he had fixed on their direction.

Moving swiftly but with caution, he proceeded toward

the source of those alluring sounds. The lobby lay behind him, which assured him that the voices had to be those of hostages who had escaped. If they were Cuban soldiers prowling through the hotel corridors, Yazid believed they should be speaking Spanish, yet another language alien and strange.

Creeping along the corridor, he tried to think how many voices there had been. Two, certainly, by definition, to permit a conversation. But Yazid was sure that one voice had been higher-pitched than those he heard at first.

A woman's voice?

Three hostages?

If he could kill them, it might please Muhunnad. Perhaps. Or, at this point, would Muhunnad prefer their heads as trophies?

Yazid did not flinch from the prospect, but he had no knife or other cutting tool. He could not sever one head, much less three, without a blade. And dragging three corpses to the lobby was impossible. It would require three trips, assuming he had strength enough to shift them all.

Assuming that Muhunnad did not kill him on the spot for breaking off his search of the hotel, without specific orders to return.

Were the speakers moving? All the better if they were, particularly if they moved in his direction. He'd surprise them, cut them down without a word of warning in the pristine hotel corridor.

Moving away? No problem. He would find them soon enough, if they were careless, speaking out of turn.

The closing-door sound troubled him, however. If they'd found a place to hide, speaking their last before they ducked inside and locked the door behind them, he could spend hours scouting through the halls.

Allah provides, he told himself. I will not fail.

THE DEADLINE WAS UPON THEM, give or take a minute, when a sound of rushing footsteps up ahead brought the Executioner to a crouching halt. Santos dropped beside him, leveling her captured weapon toward the point where their run met another corridor.

Their target burst around the corner seconds later, saw them and reacted instantly. Instead of ducking backward, he kept running in the same direction he'd been headed when they met, unleashing wild fire from his Uzi along the way.

Bolan went prone, Santos rolling off and to her left away from him, while bullets sizzled overhead. A couple smacked into the wall, inches above his prostrate form, scoring the wallpaper. Bolan was tracking for a shot but didn't get it in the time he had, before his sprinting target disappeared.

Ghulam Yazid.

Even in the traumatic circumstances, one glimpse of the grinning face had been enough. Bolan remembered the Pakistani from Brognola's file of mug shots, knew that he was dangerous—but hadn't known the man was insane until he saw that smile.

There was no sound of running footsteps now. What did it mean?

Was Yazid standing just around the corner with his Uzi poised to riddle anyone he saw? Or was he slowly creeping down the east-west corridor, escaping while they both lay huddled on the floor?

Can't risk it, Bolan thought, vaulting to his feet. Santos mimicked him, rising, but he saw no conviction in her face as their eyes met.

Bolan moved closer to the intersection of two hallways, urging Santos behind him with glances and gestures. She followed silent orders, clutching her AKSU in a white-knuckled death grip.

There was nothing for it but a rush around the corner, firing, ducking high and low in hopes Yazid would panic, missing one or both of them. Low man had better chances of survival, but the only way to give the woman that slot was to send her first.

Low man was always first.

Unless…

Bolan was working on a variation of the theme, knowing he had no time for complicated changes in the plan. Around the corner, out of sight, a door opened and someone shouted, "Hey, asshole! What's up?"

That voice…

The Uzi's rattle smothered it, and Bolan knew this was his chance. He lunged around the corner, firing, rolling over, firing once again. Santos was behind him, spraying bullets from a crouch, not bothering to roll.

Yazid was turning back to face them when they riddled him, cut spindly legs from underneath him, dropped him thrashing to the bloodied carpet. In another beat, the twitching stopped and he was done.

Bolan lay waiting, rifle steady, for the man who had assisted them to show himself. A moment later, twenty feet away, a door swung slowly open and a man's voice asked, "Is it safe?"

"For now," Bolan replied. And he was standing when Joe Danforth stepped around the open door, all smiles.

"One down," Danforth remarked.

Santos frowned, pointing behind them to the office where they'd first met Danforth, moments earlier. "How did you—?"

"They're connected," Danforth interrupted her. "Back doors and folding walls. It's like a maze in here."

"Okay," Bolan replied. "Thanks for the help. But now, stay out of sight. We don't want any accidents."

Even as Bolan spoke, Danforth came forward, stooping to retrieve Yazid's Uzi and pluck a spare magazine from the dead man's pocket.

"No more accidents," he said, retreating to the doorway from which he'd emerged. "Good luck."

The door swung shut behind him, leaving Bolan and Santos with the dead man.

13

Asim Ben Muhunnad recognized the cloying feel of panic well enough. It was, if not a wholly new sensation for him, one that had not troubled him for many years as he took part in the armed struggle of his people.

Strangely, it was not the thought of death that panicked him, but rather indecision. That was new, a vile affliction that had only plagued Muhunnad for the past few hours, as his time ran out and his men started disappearing, one by one.

That wasn't strictly true, of course. They hadn't simply disappeared. He'd sent them off on vital errands—scouting, or retrieving hostages—and none had yet returned. That didn't mean all four of them were dead.

Muhunnad needed reassurance, and in all the world he knew of only one man who could offer it. No, make that one man he could reach by telephone. As for the rest, they were in no position to receive his calls.

Retreating to the check-in counter's relative privacy, Muhunnad freed the sat phone from his belt, snapped it open and thumbed out the digits he had memorized.

No speed-dial, he had been reminded time and time again, until he grew sick of the words themselves. As if they bore a curse.

No speed-dial, but they hadn't said no calls, only be *circumspect.* A fancy word Muhunnad translated as "cautious."

But the time for caution was far past. Muhunnad needed advice on what he should do next, how he should phrase the bulletin if he decided to ignore the former deadlines and annihilate his captives all at once.

His master's distant telephone rang once, twice, then a strong, familiar voice came on the line. "Hello?"

"I need your help," Muhunnad said without preamble.

"Oh?"

"We have intruders inside the hotel! And I've lost four—no, five—five men."

"That sounds like carelessness."

"I mean, they're—"

"Say no more!" the other snapped. "Why have you called?"

"To tell you that," Muhunnad answered. "And to ask what I should do."

"We have discussed that. It is all arranged."

"But not like this!" Muhunnad hissed into the mouthpiece. "There is no time to complete the action as we meant to."

"You say that, yet you live. Stay with the plan."

Muhunnad recognized the stern tone of command, knew he should stop—even apologize—and yet he said, "You do not understand!"

"I understand that you should not have called me here. Remember your commitment and be true."

The line went dead, a static whisper in his ear reminding Muhunnad that the connection had been lost somewhere in space. Another modern miracle.

He closed the phone, set it on the shiny surface of the registration desk and checked his wristwatch. It was time to choose the next ten hostages and execute them, if he meant to follow orders.

But if he decided to rebel...

What did his leaders really know about the situation in

which Muhunnad now found himself? Would they prefer that he kill only ten more prisoners, before the soldiers burst upon him and he lost the chance to slaughter more?

If they refused to listen, out of arrogance or for some other reason, it became his duty as commander on the scene to make adjustments, change his tactics to accommodate the circumstances.

Muhunnad caught his surviving soldiers, the Afghan and the Egyptian, watching him. Neither called out to ask what he was thinking, what the phone call was about, but both wore watches and had to know the deadline had elapsed.

Muhunnad beckoned them, watching the huddled prisoners as the men joined him. Without seeking direction they flanked him, keeping their eyes and weapons trained upon the hostages.

"The time has come," he told them solemnly, "to change our plan."

THE EXECUTIONER did not inquire into the woman's feelings after she had helped him kill Ghulam Yazid. He'd heard Santos firing, saw her bullets strike the terrorist along with his, and knew she had to be feeling something from her first kill, but they didn't have the time to sit around and psychoanalyze.

If Bolan's watch was correct—and he had no reason to doubt it—they were already on borrowed time.

"We should be hearing it," Santos said, while keeping pace beside him. "More killing, now. It's overdue."

"Maybe our shooting threw them off," Bolan replied. "Maybe they've got a new plan working."

"How far?" he asked, wishing once again that there'd been time and opportunity to study floor plans.

"If we could walk through walls, another hundred feet," she said. "This way."

Bolan recalled Joe Danforth's words: Back doors and folding

walls. It's like a maze in here. They might duck into any shop or office they passed along the way, cut through the passages connecting rooms, beyond the view of paying guests—

And get lost in the maze.

He knew shortcuts on unfamiliar ground could lead to trouble, even sudden death. The odds were long enough against them as it was, without departing from a sure path onto one that might lead nowhere.

"We'll be in time," she said, as if consoling him.

Bolan almost asked for what, but kept it to himself. He answered her with silence and kept moving.

Toward the killing ground.

How long before the Cuban soldiers heard enough and gave up waiting on the sidelines? If they crashed the party after Bolan and Santos were engaged with Muhunnad's commandos, it would be a bloody mess, with emphasis on *bloody*.

Should they cut and run, in that case? Try to make it clear before the place was sealed, or keep on fighting? When the soldiers came, they wouldn't be in any mood for sorting out combatants. It would be a case of kill 'em all and let God sort 'em out.

Pausing briefly at another corner, checking out the corridor beyond in preparation for his move, he turned and asked Santos, "Can you do this?"

She considered it, not asking what he meant, and then nodded. "Yes. I can."

"Okay," he said, accepting it. "Be ready. We're almost there."

"WHEN DO WE KILL THEM, then?" Parwana asked.

"Ten minutes more," Muhunnad replied. "If there is no response by then, watch for my signal and commence to fire."

"Or, we could kill them now," Parwana said.

"I have explained that," Muhunnad reminded him. "Outside, they heard the shooting and grenades already. They believe that we have met the last deadline. Now, they have one last chance to answer our demands."

"You think they will?" The question came from Uthman, standing on Muhunnad's left.

The leader shrugged. "It's possible." His tone and attitude said otherwise.

Parwana understood that they had ten, perhaps fifteen minutes left to live.

It was a heady feeling, knowing when his mortal life would end and he would make the leap to Paradise. After the endless prayers and sermons, dreams and theoretical discussions, plans and schemes, it came to him as a relief. From the cradle up, his thirty-one years had been hard ones. Giving up his earthly life at last would be no sacrifice, to speak of.

"So, ten minutes, then," he said.

"Ten minutes," Muhunnad confirmed.

"And if they come before then?" Parwana asked.

"If who comes?"

"Whoever's killing off the others. I'm not deaf, you know." A little insubordination did not harm, Parwana reckoned, in the final quarter hour of his life.

"We don't know anyone's been killed," Muhunnad said, somehow retaining a straight face.

"One of the guns, at least, was wrong," Parwana answered. "Not Kalashnikov, and not 9 mm."

"So? What would you have me do? Are you prepared to go and find the answer? Shall *I* go, and leave you here?" Muhunnad's anger left him trembling.

Parwana shrugged again. "I simply asked what happens if they come before you give the signal," he replied.

"What do you *think* happens?" Muhunnad asked them both.

"We kill the hostages?" Uthman suggested.

"Yes! Praise Allah! Are we clear on the procedure, now?"

"You give the signal, we kill hostages," Uthman said. "Enemies attack us, we kill hostages."

"Perfect! Go back and take your places now. Let none among the captives recognize our plan."

As if they haven't got a clue by now, Parwana thought, but said nothing.

Most of the hostages were watching their three captors, tracking Uthman and Parwana as they moved back to their places at the points of an imaginary triangle. Only a blind man or a fool could fail to grasp the meaning of their placement, covering the huddled mass of prisoners.

Parwana wondered why the whole lot of them had not bolted when the others fled. They'd missed their last chance at survival, let it slip between their fingers—why? For fear of being killed or injured?

Now, because they had been timid, all of them would die.

That thought, his vision of the great bloodletting soon to bless him, made Bahram Parwana smile.

"WE SHOULD BE ALMOST THERE," Santos said.

Her whisper sounded like a shout to Bolan, made him grimace at the thought that someone else might hear her and spring out at them from hiding.

Now that he knew for certain that hostages had managed to escape and were at large in the hotel, roaming about with nothing that resembled leadership or strategy, each move he made was doubly fraught with peril.

Some of those who had escaped were armed with weapons taken from their captors, others possibly with tools and implements procured from the hotel itself. They would be frightened, furious, in no mood to ask questions if they met a stranger prowling through the corridors. Surprise distractions and attacks were definitely possible, as Joe Danforth had demonstrated.

Anyone could spring upon them now, from anywhere, at any time.

"I said—"

"I heard you," Bolan answered.

"Sorry!" she muttered, then fell silent.

She was right, he realized. They had to be getting close. Bolan glanced down to check his Steyr's plastic magazine, deciding on the spot to switch it out for one fully loaded. Santos watched and followed his example. Bolan's sidearm, still untouched since landing, had a full magazine with a live round up the spout, and Bolan still had all but one of the grenades he'd carried with him from the beach.

They were as ready as they'd ever be to meet their enemies.

They crept along the final stretch of corridor in single file, Santos watching out behind them as she followed Bolan's lead. Two agonizing minutes later, Bolan found that he'd run out of cover, as the hallway spit them out into a sunken area complete with stage, tables and sofas, where a small band could set up and entertain an audience of twenty-five or thirty guests.

The lobby lay beyond that modest amphitheater. Bolan glimpsed bodies massed together there, seated in folding chairs or on the floor, before he ducked into the pit. Santos followed, nearly stumbling on the steps, but caught herself short of a noisy fall.

They scuttled side-by-side across the sunken space, then crept up the opposing steps until they had a mole's-eye view of the lobby proper. The Executioner scanned the scene in front of him and quickly gave up counting hostages. They were too closely packed, many obscured by those seated in front of them. He couldn't tell—might never know—how many had escaped before he reached the scene.

In any case, the shooters were his first priority.

Bolan saw two of them, and understood from darting hostage eyes that there had to be at least one more beyond his line of sight, concealed within the angle where a gift shop thrust into the lobby on his right. Three automatic weapons, anyway, positioned for a deadly cross fire, none more than five or six yards from the nearest targets.

How could the shooters miss at that range?

Bolan reckoned it would be impossible. Even a dying burst, unaimed, could kill or wound a dozen hostages before the triggerman went down. If one of them was tough enough to hold the trigger down for a full magazine, with armor-piercing military rounds, the damage could be thirty dead or more.

Bolan needed something in the way of shock and awe.

Frowning, his eyes locked on the tableau before him, Bolan reached to his belt for a rifle grenade.

ISHAQ UTHMAN WAS GETTING nervous as his time ran out. His life was coming to an end, that much he knew and had accepted, but the damned infernal waiting nearly drove him mad.

Uthman's emotions had come full-circle in the course of twenty-four hours. First, he had experienced relief and something close to ecstasy, at being liberated from his cage at Camp X-Ray. Next came the fear of fleeing under fire from the Marines who'd guarded him since his arrest and transfer to Guantanamo. More joy when he'd escaped unscathed, then something close to shock when he was told that he'd been liberated to join in a glorious suicide mission. Finally, acceptance, as he came to terms with the assignment and looked forward to the thrills of Paradise.

But now, the nerves were back.

Uthman paced restlessly, watching the hostages and shooting glances toward the two comrades remaining from their team of eight. Nearly two-thirds already gone, before they even faced the enemy.

Uthman believed that he was ready for the end. He had no family, few friends who would remember him from better days. If he died well, perhaps—

The muffled shot came from his left, somewhere beyond his line of sight. Uthman was turning toward the sound when something happened to the lobby's ceiling. Stricken by a smoky thunderclap, a great piece of it crumbled, raining down around Asim Ben Muhunnad.

Recoiling from the powerful explosion, Uthman took a moment to regain his senses. This was it! The final showdown he had waited for and steeled his nerves against.

His first duty, in the event of an attack, was to annihilate the hostages. They huddled in a trembling mass before him now, most of them screaming, weeping, but the Egyptian hesitated.

There would be more honor in his death, Uthman believed, if he died fighting other men of arms. They'd be upon him any moment, and he didn't want to meet them with an empty rifle, fumbling with a backup magazine, while unarmed corpses cooled around his feet.

A glance showed Muhunnad still alive and struggling to his feet, covered with plaster dust that turned his dusky skin and jet-black hair the pasty white of corpse flesh. Closer, but still thirty feet away from Uthman's post, Bahram Parwana pressed a palm against his forehead, then examined bloody fingers.

Still alive and evidently fit to fight, all three of them. Uthman held his Kalashnikov still pointed at the screaming hostages, but did not fire. Parwana, likewise, aimed no shots into the crowd, but rather turned in the direction of the shot Uthman had heard before the ceiling burst and fell.

There was no bullet that could cause a ceiling to explode. His thoughts were shattered in a heartbeat, as another pop came from somewhere to his left, followed immediately by a second blast that took a giant bite out of the marble registration desk.

The shock wave from that detonation punched the air from Uthman's lungs and sent him sprawling to the floor.

"READY?" BOLAN ASKED, with the echo of his two grenades still ringing in his ears.

Santos bobbed her head in the affirmative, grim-faced and tense, the only way to be, right now.

"Let's go!" Bolan said, up and running even as he spoke. A pair of indoor palm trees blocked his view of one shooter who'd fallen when the ceiling caved, but he could see enough to get him started.

Near the middle of the rubble pile, Asim Ben Muhunnad was on his feet and shouting to his men in Arabic. He hadn't started firing at the hostages, but when he did—

Bolan stopped short and raised his AUG, Santos sliding to a halt beside him as he drew a bead on Muhunnad. Before Bolan could fire, though, bullets from another quarter filled the air around him, sending him into a dive-and-roll that saved his life, but spoiled his killing shot.

The shots that saved Muhunnad's life had come from Bolan's right, the blind spot near the hotel's gift shop that had worried him on his approach. Slick tile beneath him, Bolan slithered for the nearest cover, which turned out to be the potted palms.

It wasn't much, but soil packed into heavy terra cotta pots served as a kind of sandbag barrier against incoming rounds. Bolan heard bullets strike the pots and slap the palm trunks overhead. A second automatic weapon joined the chorus, spraying slugs around his hiding place.

Keep at it, Bolan thought. The more rounds fired at him,

the less his enemies would have to spare for hostages when Bolan made his move.

And what would that be, from his present situation?

He looked around and saw Santos sprawled behind some kind of pamphlet rack she'd overturned, spilling its brightly colored contents like confetti on the polished lobby floor.

The setup didn't offer protection from the bullets fired by military weapons. Half a dozen rounds had already punched through it, but as far as he could tell, they hadn't struck her prostrate form.

As if in answer to his silent inquiry, she peeked around the nearest corner of her flimsy barricade, flashed him a smile, then ducked back out of sight.

To help her out, Bolan fired a short burst between the arching palms above him, angling toward the ruin of the central lobby's ceiling. Wood and plaster there should stop his rounds without producing ricochets.

More squealing from the hostages with each round fired, but none of them were hit so far, from what Bolan could tell. Their would-be killers were distracted for the moment, but it wouldn't last.

If Muhunnad's guerrillas failed to take out Bolan and Santos in the next few moments, at least one of them was bound to turn upon the hostages with raking fire.

Huddled behind the giant terra cotta pots, Bolan unclipped another flash-bang from his belt and yanked the pin. It was a risky move for all concerned, but if he didn't do something, and quickly, all the hazards he had faced so far might be in vain.

More bullets chipped the pots that sheltered him, spilled dirt and peat moss to the lobby floor. The stout trunks of the palms spewed ragged chips of bark with fiber strings attached, as slugs gnawed into them.

Clutching the stun grenade, Bolan lay waiting for a lull in

hostile fire that would permit his pitch. One little break was all he needed, just a heartbeat.

When it came, he snarled and gave the long toss everything he had, then ducked back under cover as a new storm broke around him, deadly hail careening off the lobby's smooth tile floor.

14

Captain Raul Cervantes and his twenty men were huddled in the shadows of the hotel's loading dock, when sounds of full-scale battle echoed from inside. One of his men was working on the access door, picking its lock by the illumination of a flashlight beam, when an explosion rocked the place, immediately followed by a storm of automatic fire.

Cervantes pulled the kneeling corporal away from his unfinished task and barked an order at the others to stand clear. Taking position ten feet from the door, Cervantes leveled his Kalashnikov and blew its locks apart with half a dozen 7.62 mm Soviet rounds.

A kick cleared the doorway, and they were inside. Another loud explosion briefly interrupted the reports of small-arms fire, telling Cervantes where his team needed to be.

He had shunned the direct approach that would have had them blasting through the lobby doors and windows, while their targets used the hostages as human shields. Now, listening to screams and gunfire from that very lobby, he could only wonder if they were too late.

Cervantes would not let himself believe it, not until he saw the evidence with his own eyes. And if he saw it, if his soldiers were confronted with a wholesale slaughter of the innocents, the fate of those who'd killed the captives would be sealed.

No prisoners.

Although Cervantes thought himself humane, within the limits of his chosen profession, he believed that certain evils ought to be exterminated root and branch, before they had a chance to spread. If global terrorists believed they had a friend in Cuba—*his* Cuba—the captain meant to show them that they were fatally mistaken.

Cervantes sent two scouts, then led the other eighteen men through winding corridors. The hotel seemed much larger than it had when he was standing in the outer darkness, looking for a way inside. Cervantes feared they might be lost, then saw directions on the wall and realized they couldn't miss the fight if they just followed its explosive sounds.

When they were roughly halfway there, his scouts stopped short, aiming their rifles at a clutch of men and women who had suddenly appeared before them, spilling from the open doorway of what seemed to be a storage room. One of the men dropped a rifle when he saw the soldiers, stretching full length on the floor before they had a chance to throw him down. The others stood with hands raised overhead, three women and two men.

Not terrorists, Cervantes quickly realized. Pale skins and frightened eyes, two of the men babbling excited English in a bid to save themselves. Cervantes snatched the AKSU rifle from its place beside the prostrate man, and had his soldiers hoist the gunman to his feet.

"Who are you?" he demanded of the man who'd held the rifle, while he held the gun between them. "Where did you get this?"

"Joe Danforth," the prisoner said. "I'm a—we're all guests here, at the resort." He nodded toward the AKSU, saying, "I took that from one of *them*. The terrorists."

Cervantes frowned. "And how did you disarm him, Señor Danforth?

"Hey, it wasn't me, okay?" Danforth replied. "I mean, I

helped, okay? Got lucky and distracted him. The others wasted him, and I picked up the gun."

"Others? What do you mean, others?"

"Like you guys," Danforth said. "Well, not exactly. Not in uniform, or anything. The lady had a swimsuit on. Now, that's an image I won't soon forget, believe me. And I want to say the man was in a wet suit, like some kind of diver."

Diver? Wet suit? Lady?

"Were they Cuban?" Cervantes asked.

"I'm not sure. She might've been, I guess. The man spoke English and he looked…I don't know…more Italian, if I had to guess."

"Where did they go?"

"I didn't stay around to watch," Danforth said, then his eyes flicked toward the sounds of battle. "But my guess would be, they went to join the party."

ASIM BEN MUHUNNAD lurched through an obscuring haze of smoke and plaster dust. He was excited, angry, frightened and bewildered, all at once. His fingers fumbled with the empty magazine from his Kalashnikov, then dropped it, somehow managing to put a fresh one in its place.

No sooner was the gun reloaded than he fired a burst across the hotel lobby—not toward the assembled, wailing hostages, but toward the muzzle-flashes of advancing hostile guns.

Who were these enemies? Why did it seem to Muhunnad that there were only two of them so far?

The twin explosions, bringing down the lobby ceiling and demolishing the check-in desk, made him think the Cuban army had invaded the hotel. Even before the echoes of the first blast cleared his head, however, Muhunnad had seen two strange, astounding figures rushing toward him, firing automatic weapons as they ran.

A man dressed all in black, like a commando…and a *woman in a bathing suit?*

Muhunnad had considered that he might be suffering hallucinations from head trauma, but his enemies—whoever or whatever they might be—were definitely firing at him, charging him as if they had a hundred troops behind them. Muhunnad heard bullets snapping past his head, striking the wall behind him, ricocheting into space.

New hope flared in Muhunnad's chest as concentrated fire from Uthman and Parwana drove both targets under cover, the man behind a looming pair of potted palms, the woman sprawled behind a flimsy rack of tourist pamphlets toppled on its side. The trees and massive terra cotta pots were proving difficult to crack, even with automatic rifle fire, but Muhunnad was confident the woman would be dead or wounded in a minute, maybe less.

He thought so, until Uthman and Parwana broke off firing to reload their weapons almost simultaneously. Then, while Muhunnad pumped short bursts from his AKSU toward the woman's flimsy cover, something flickered at the corner of his eye.

A waving arm, perhaps? What sense did that make?

Glancing to his left, Muhunnad saw an object more or less the size and shape of a soup can, tumbling toward him through the air. He was turning, breaking for the cover of the shattered registration desk, before the canister bounced once on impact with the tile beneath his feet.

The first two blasts had both been loud enough. Muhunnad might have said ear-shattering, except that he still had some vestige of his hearing left, returning by degrees. He lost it when the next, truly apocalyptic blast enveloped him, plucked him off his feet and punched him through an awkward tumbling somersault.

He landed deaf and blind, flat on his back, the air mashed from his lungs as if a giant hand had squeezed his chest. Muhunnad fought to draw a breath, while wallowing in rubble like an overturned tortoise. By the time he finally remembered how to breathe *and* walk, Muhunnad realized that he had lost his rifle.

No matter. He still had a pistol and grenades, securely fastened to his belt. Jerking into a semblance of an upright stance, Muhunnad drew his automatic pistol from its dusty holster with his right hand, thumbing back its hammer, while his left hand groped along his belt for a grenade.

"I'm ready for you!" he called out in Arabic. "You want me? Here I am!"

ISHAQ UTHMAN SAW SPOTS before his eyes —or were the spots inside his eyes? He had been facing toward the open lobby, from the general direction of the shattered check-in desk, when the concussion bomb exploded thirty feet in front of him. The white-hot light seemed to sear his retinas, while giant hands slapped both his ears at once, and he was cast onto a pile of rubble by the blast's shock wave.

Aching, stone-deaf and nearly blind, the young Egyptian had managed to retain his weapon. It was all he had in these, the final moments of his life, and he was not about to let it go.

Movement was agony, but Uthman forced himself to move, one aching, palsied joint after another. Using his Kalashnikov as a short crutch, until his quaking legs could bear his weight, Uthman stood and let a remnant of the blasted registration desk support his sagging form.

Where were his two unlikely enemies, the man and woman he had tried to kill, and who had nearly killed him in return?

From where he stood, Uthman could see behind the toppled pamphlet rack. The woman had escaped, and he assumed the man had also gone to ground elsewhere. A sudden sense of being watched made him duck his head and stumble through a wide gap in the middle of the check-in counter, seeking cover in its shadow.

He was safer there, undoubtedly. Leaning across the desk, his AK braced atop it, he could sweep most of the lobby when the interlopers showed themselves.

What of the hostages?

Incredibly, most of them still huddled where they'd been before the gunfire and explosions started. Many of them were facedown on the floor, arms covering their heads, in ranks that brought to mind street scenes of mass arrests in his homeland.

Why don't they run? he asked himself, then spoke the words aloud. "Why don't you run?"

No answer from the people on the floor—perhaps because the blasts had deafened them, maybe because he spoke a language none of them could understand.

Uthman was tempted to start shooting them, find out if that would make the strange invaders show themselves. Just one or two, to start, saving his ammunition for the main event.

It would be simple, leaning just a little farther out from where he stood, angling the AKSU's muzzle downward, with the weapon set for semiautomatic fire. It didn't even matter if he killed the hostages he shot, as long as others started screaming louder, to attract their would-be saviors.

Ishaq Uthman didn't see the stun grenades in flight, pitched one after another from behind the concierge's desk, some forty feet away. He was selecting targets, had a fat man in his sights, when suddenly the world went white again and he was slammed against the nearest wall.

MARIA SANTOS WAITED for the double blast from Cooper's last two stun grenades, her eyes tightly closed, hands clasped over her ringing ears. Unsure how many more shocks she could stand, she was determined nonetheless to follow Cooper where he led in one last charge against their enemies.

Or, more precisely, to obey his orders and not follow where he led.

She understood his strategy, splitting the two of them and sending her off to the left, while he went to the right and faced the greater danger. It was not an insult, since he clearly had the greater confidence and skill.

If she could stop one of the three remaining terrorists before he started killing hostages, she would accept congratulations for a job well done.

Assuming she was still alive, and not locked up in prison.

There would be no congratulations from the military or the state security police, of course. Only a cage and truncheons, water and electrodes, pain and screams before she——

The explosions saved her from imagining her own prolonged and ghastly death. They came almost together, rocked her in her crouch behind the concierge's desk, then she felt Cooper slap her on the shoulder, telling her that it was time to go.

She bolted up and through the swinging gate, around the horseshoe counter to her left. Cooper would vault the counter, naturally, but she didn't watch him do it, focused absolutely on her destination and whoever might attempt to keep her from it.

And at first, there seemed to be no one. The lobby swirled with smoke and dust in front of her, still echoing with the concussive blasts of Cooper's stun grenades. The hostages were wailing, moaning, well off to her right, but that was Cooper's killing zone.

Just when she thought the twin explosions might have cleared all opposition from her path, a lanky figure caked with plaster dust appeared, lurching out of the haze and brandishing a weapon very like her own.

Santos fired instinctively and missed, her target sidestepping or stumbling on debris from one of the explosions, either diving to the floor or simply falling. Either way, she missed, and that was all that mattered.

As he fell, the gunman fired a short burst of his own. An accident? Deliberately? The bullets rattled past her, inches from her left arm.

It was her turn to drop and roll, dodging her adversary's line of fire. Untrained as Santos was in close-quarters combat—or any other kind, for that matter—she still avoided taking any hits when the tumbling terrorist fired once again, from the floor.

It struck her as preposterous, almost enough to make her laugh, two people rolling on the hotel lobby's tile with guns, no more than twenty feet apart. She might have laughed, if it was not so deadly serious.

This stranger meant to kill her, and in order to survive, she had to kill him first.

Screaming in rage, Santos stopped rolling and held down the AK's trigger, firing off half a magazine in one long burst. Her enemy recoiled from the explosive impact of incoming rounds, his face imploding, the crown of his skull lifting off, while his body jerked and shuddered spastically.

Enough!

He was beyond dead, but the danger from his comrades still remained. More gunfire echoed through the lobby, overriding screams from frightened hostages…and something else.

From somewhere in the middle distance, she heard voices drawing nearer. Make that one voice, snapping out commands in military fashion.

Soldiers!

She turned to look for Cooper, was about to call his name in warning, when the impact of a bullet sent her spinning to the floor.

MUHUNNAD SAW Ishaq Uthman die, his face obliterated by a stream of bullets from the nearly naked woman's AKSU rifle. Blinking gritty plaster dust and choking on the smoke that filled his nostrils, Muhunnad still wondered if he might be hallucinating, but he did not hesitate. Raising his pistol as the woman turned to face him, squeezing off a hasty round, he watched her jerk and fall.

The stunning impact cut Muhunnad's legs from under him. He fell, rolled desperately for cover in the rubble of the former registration desk, while gunfire and the screams of hostages resounded in his ears.

Muhunnad knew he had been shot somewhere below the waist, but could not isolate the wound. Crawling, he found his right leg functional, the left a deadweight trailing on the floor behind him. That much told him bones were broken, either in the leg itself, or in his hip. It took another moment for the pain to register, but he had found a little cover then and ground his teeth to keep the whining sounds inside himself.

The man in black had shot him, obviously. Muhunnad had seen him, charging like a spectral figure toward Parwana's hiding place beside the hotel gift shop, when the nearly naked harlot had appeared, dueling with Uthman, killing him. Her body and her weapon had distracted Muhunnad, and even as he killed her, her companion had a chance to strike.

So be it, the grizzled Palestinian thought. We all came here to die.

But he could kill more infidels before that happened, maybe even drop the man who'd wounded him.

The hostages were in a panic now, all frenzied noise and stirring where they'd been corralled for hours. Several had already fled on foot, ducking the cross fire that surrounded them, but most had lost their nerve after the first revolt. They might have cringed before Muhunnad's guns forever, but the battle raging in their midst now made a crucial difference. If they saw any reasonable opportunity to flee…

Three dashed across the littered floor in front of him, even as he formed his thought. Two men, each gripped one arm of a woman who could not keep pace with them, half-dragging her along, sometimes lifting her feet clear of the floor.

Muhunnad chased them with a pistol shot and missed, then cursed himself for wasting precious ammunition. What if Allah had intended that one bullet for the man in black?

Muhunnad felt as if his mind was drifting on a tide of dizziness and pain. From somewhere in the middle distance, he heard shouting, all male voices, issuing and answering commands. It brought back memories of training camps in Lebanon and Syria, but otherwise the voices made no sense to him.

One man obsessed him, and Muhunnad saw him now, emerging from the shadows where another crumpled form—Parwana?—sprawled in death. The grim-faced man was coming for him.

A real man would go out to meet him, Muhunnad thought.

Using his left arm and his right leg to propel him, humming as an antidote to screams, Muhunnad struck a precarious half-kneeling posture, using both hands as a brace for his pistol.

He tracked the wet-suited target, firing two, three rounds before the man in black squeezed off a short burst from his weapon. Even as the bullets stitched across his midsection, Muhunnad recognized the gunshots he'd heard earlier—the weapon that was out of place.

Case solved, he thought, sprawled on his back, eyes staring at the ruined ceiling as the light began to fade. At least, his legs no longer hurt as badly now. Of course, he couldn't move them, but he thought it was a decent trade.

A thousand rushing feet, it seemed, were shaking the very floor beneath him. Straining for a glance along the bloodied ruin of his body, Muhunnad saw a virtual stampede of hostages approaching, driven mad at last.

Muhunnad closed his eyes, began another silent prayer before the crazed mob trampled him and left him broken in its wake.

MARIA SANTOS LAY where she had fallen, dropped by a pistol shot. The Executioner was half expecting her to have no pulse, but when he knelt beside her, she reached out to clutch his sleeve and rasped, "Soldiers!"

"I know," he answered. "This will hurt."

She couldn't help much as he jostled her into position for a fireman's carry, lifting with his legs, clutching the Steyr's pistol grip in his right hand. A grunt of pain told Bolan that his estimate had been correct.

It hurt, but she was still alive.

The Cuban troops were nearly there. He couldn't see them yet, a saving grace, but he could hear them calling back and forth in Spanish, no pretense of stealth with all the gunfire thereabouts. A backward glance showed Bolan that the bulk of fleeing hostages had run in that direction, toward their khaki-clad saviors, which could only slow the soldiers.

So far, so good.

He headed in the opposite direction, past the ruin of the check-in desk, ducked through the hotel manager's preserve, and came out in another corridor where signs directed him to outdoor facilities.

Santos grunted something at him, had to try a second time before he understood her. "I can walk."

"We need to run," Bolan replied, and gripped her legs more tightly where they draped across his left shoulder.

"Feel sick," she gasped.

"Don't fight it," Bolan said. "The wet suit's waterproof."

He found the exit moments later, hit the push bar with his

right hip, shouldered through and got them both outside. Most of the outer lights were dark, from preset timers or some action by the Cuban military.

Either way, it helped.

Bolan ran on, bearing the woman's weight, until they were two hundred yards from the hotel and well concealed on wooded grounds. It seemed impossible that they had missed the Cuban soldiers altogether, but if someone in command had picked a special hostage-rescue team, the others might be hanging back, giving the specialists a chance.

He set Santos on her feet, leaning against a tree, and used a penlight to inspect her shoulder wound. She had full movement in her arm, although it made her groan through gritted teeth. No broken bones, then, and a compress would control the bleeding long enough for her to reach a hospital.

But first, they had to reach her car.

And that meant swimming.

That meant sharks, if any of her blood soaked through the gauze and left a scent trail in the water.

"Leave me," she said.

"No way," he replied.

"It is the *only* way."

"You've been shot once," Bolan reminded her. "I will not leave you to a firing squad."

"Why would they shoot an injured guest of the hotel?" she asked him.

"Say again?"

"Take all the weapons with you. Drop them anywhere you like. I was returning from the hotel's swimming pool and met the terrorists. One of them wounded me, but I escaped. Simple."

"It won't be simple, when the soldiers check your name against the register, or if they want to see your room."

"You overestimate them," she replied. "They are conditioned to regard women as weak and helpless. By the time they finish celebrating their great victory over the terrorists, they won't know where to find me."

It made sense, but Bolan hesitated, glancing back at the hotel. Another sputtering of gunfire told him that the soldiers had arrived and were engaged in mopping up their lifeless enemies.

"All right," he said at last, unbuckling her belt and scooping up the magazines that tumbled from it. "What about your pistol?"

"It's not registered," she said.

"You're sure about this?" he demanded.

"Go!" she said. "Before it is too late."

He went, and left the gutsy woman standing in the darkness, covering his back.

15

Washington, D.C.

Another long day at the Saudi embassy made Nabi Ulmal-hama happy to come home, relax, unwind. For two straight days he had been fielding media inquiries on the incidents in Cuba, offering his nation's sympathy to all the victims and their loved ones, reassuring everyone within the sound of his correctly solemn voice that no one in the Saudi government had any knowledge of the terrorist attacks beyond what was reported by the press in Washington or from Havana.

Granted, those accounts of the events were often contradictory. Cuban reporters charged that the United States had planned the raids, placed specially trained commandos at Guantanamo Bay, then staged their "escape" to unleash a reign of terror on the Democratic People's Republic of Cuba.

Within twelve hours of the final killing spree at Bahia Matanzas, the U.S. media had publicly identified most of the guerrillas involved in that raid and the sinking of the *Tropic Princess*. Survivors from the Cuban slaughter and relatives of victims lost in both attacks monopolized the network morning shows, while talking heads on Court TV debated the potential benefits of international lawsuits against Allah's Warriors.

Ulmalhama found solace in whiskey, regretting that the exercise he'd planned had not been a complete success. It had been glorious, watching the cruise ship sink with most of those on board, fewer than one in five escaping from the blasted hulk as it slipped underneath the waves.

As for Bahia Matanzas…

He would never have a chance to question Asim Ben Muhunnad to find out why so many hostages were left alive, when Cuban troops invaded the resort. Muhunnad should have slaughtered them at the first intimation of a rescue, using every weapon in his arsenal, but something had gone hideously wrong.

Early reports from Cuba indicated that Muhunnad's men were scattered, one found dead at some distance from the hotel itself, while several others died at various points around the ground floor, well removed from the lobby and most of the hostages. Worse yet, it was reported that many of the captives had escaped *before* the Cuban troops arrived to liberate them, even seizing weapons from Muhunnad's men.

It was disgusting, a display of gross incompetence that would have warranted Muhunnad's execution, if he hadn't been already dead.

Perhaps, he could find some of Muhunnad's relatives and punish them, instead, visit the suffering intended for their worthless kin on others, as an object lesson to Allah's Warriors officers and fighting men.

But first, the Saudi diplomat needed release from tension that the whiskey left untouched. He palmed his cell phone, dialed a Georgetown number he had memorized, and scheduled a deluxe massage to be performed at his apartment, in one hour. Yes, the operator told him, Mistress Crystal was most certainly available.

She was his favorite among the escorts and masseuses employed by the service Ulmalhama patronized twice weekly, on average. He was overdue for a release of the anxiety pent up inside him since his operation had begun.

There would be questions when he met next with the organization's commanders, but they should be mollified to some extent by the publicity their movement had received. Such incidents boosted recruiting and donations, even if their goals were not entirely realized.

Besides, he told himself, in some respects they *had* triumphed. The death toll had been impressive, while Washington was shown up as a paper tiger, weak and ineffective. Ulmalhama's superiors might be disappointed in the body count at Bahia Matanzas, but he could still paint the effort as a media triumph of sorts.

Pleased with himself, the diplomat poured another dollop of whiskey into his glass and moved toward his bedroom. It was time to prepare for Mistress Crystal and the pleasures she would bring him in an hour's time.

Pleasures, Ulmalhama told himself, that he richly deserved for a job well done.

BROGNOLA HAD SUPPLIED the name, address, telephone numbers and a dossier on Bolan's target. They had confirmed beyond any doubt that the target had placed one call to Bahia Matanzas and received one from the same source, in the midst of the late hostage crisis.

Case closed—almost.

The target's name was Nabi Ulmalhama, a forty-two-year-old cultural attaché to the Saudi Arabian embassy in Washington. According to the file, he had no wife, no children, seemed to be the kind of public servant who was married to his work. A closer look revealed that when in Washington, he utilized the services of an escort service, taking delivery at his luxurious Georgetown flat without any inconvenience to himself.

Bolan parked his rented car on a side street, two blocks south of Ulmalhama's apartment complex and gave his gear one final check. He wore all black, from his light raincoat to his turtleneck, jeans, and the knit cap on his head that would roll down into a ski mask for his final approach.

Because he had a floor plan of the target's flat, but didn't know who might be waiting for him there, Bolan had come loaded for bear. His Beretta 93-R selective-fire pistol had a sound suppressor attached, snug in its left-armpit rig with spare magazines on the right side for balance. His Spectre submachine gun, also silenced to the best of his ability, hung from a strap over his right shoulder, hidden by the raincoat but accessible through its slit pockets. On his belt, Bolan wore a commando dagger and two flash-bang grenades.

The Executioner's extraction from the Cuban coast had gone off better then he had any right to expect. Whatever message was broadcast from the hostage-rescue team at Bahia Matanzas, it had drawn most of the troops to the hotel, leaving giant gaps in their perimeter. The beach patrols were also lax, glutted on victory, and no one had been watching when Bolan retrieved his scuba gear and swam away.

Hot wiring Maria's old car was no challenge, in the absence of any serious security devices, and Bolan had taken his time on the drive back to their original rendezvous point.

The most dangerous part was heading out to sea aboard the Zodiac inflatable raft, trusting his emergency signal transmitter to summon the *Poseidon* from wherever it was hiding, fathoms deep and safely out of sight. When it surfaced like a monster rising from the depths, Bolan had finally begun to let himself relax.

That lasted until he was back on U.S. soil, and Brognola had briefed him on the one who got away.

Make that the one who *thought* he'd get away.

It was a brisk walk to the target's complex, through a sprinkling rain that Bolan hardly noticed. Ulmalhama's hefty rent included marginal security: specifically, closed-circuit television cameras in the underground garage, and a uniformed—but unarmed—doorman who took karate classes twice a month.

Bolan ignored the underground approach and showed his FBI credentials to the doorman. They were more or less legitimate.

"The Bureau, eh? Looking for somebody?"

"Could be."

"Hey, I can tell you anything you need to know," the doorman said.

"I'll make a note," Bolan replied, and left him to patrol the sidewalk.

Ulmalhama's flat was on the fourteenth floor, one of those buildings that had no thirteenth. Bolan surveyed the empty lobby, took the elevator up to twelve and got off there to use the stairs.

Whoever might be waiting for him on the floor above, misnumbered as it was for superstition's sake, they were about to have a run of rotten luck.

THE PROSTITUTE WAS a surprise. She had to have come up in a different elevator, maybe entered the apartment building seconds behind Bolan, disembarking from the lift while he was toiling up the stairs between the twelfth and fourteenth floors.

She wore a see-through raincoat, plastic like a shower curtain. It showed a slinky little cocktail dress beneath it, black material that looked like velvet from a distance, with dark hosiery and black stilettos to match. Her hair was bottle blond, cut shoulder length.

Bolan came up behind her as she was about to knock, gave her a shoulder tap that made her turn around and gasp.

"Jesus!" she said. "You scared me. Who are you?"

He let her see the FBI credentials with his face, Matt

Cooper's name. "Your client's double-booked tonight, and doesn't know it yet. You're done."

"Funny." She offered him a wicked smile. "I don't feel done."

"And you don't want to," Bolan said.

This time, he let her see the weapon slung underneath his raincoat, and she took the hint. "I'll just be going then, shall I?" she said.

"Sounds like a good idea."

"You know, he always has at least two men there with him," she said.

"Good to know," Bolan said.

He stood and tracked her with his eyes, watching her watching him until the elevator came and she stepped into it, door hissing shut behind her. Was she pulling out her cell phone, dialing Ulmalhama's number with a warning as a parting shot?

He heard no ringing telephones behind the door in front of him, but that proved nothing. Ulmalhama had at least three bedrooms, plus a living room and kitchen, other places where a phone could ring and ring without its sounds reaching the outer hall.

He thought about the door, wondering whether he should knock, and then decided not to bother. Hauling out the submachine gun, carried with a live round in the chamber and its safety off because it had a full-time double-action trigger, Bolan ripped the doorknob and the dead bolt with a short burst that still left plenty of ammo in the little chopper's magazine.

He followed with a kick and bulled on through, knowing the guards would be in motion now, scrambling for weapons if they weren't already armed and on alert. The entryway was clear, but Bolan picked up movement in the living room that opened to his right, sofas arranged to face a huge TV set.

Bolan dropped to a crouch as two men bolted off the couch,

lurching apart as if their parents had come home and caught them playing nasty games. They both wore navy slacks and white shirts without ties, almost an in-house uniform. They had black hair and swarthy faces, each with a mustache.

The only visible distinction was their choice of holsters. Number one, on Bolan's left, had picked a shoulder rig and had to have slipped the pistol out for comfort's sake, while he was lounging on the sofa. Number two, dodging to Bolan's right had kept his sidearm in a high-rise holster, belted to his hip.

He was a lefty, going for the pistol while his partner made a quick swoop toward the nearby coffee table, doubtless going for the gun he'd laid aside. Bolan squeezed off a burst that spoiled the shooter's snow-white shirt forever, drenching it with crimson as he toppled over backward, pistol still securely holstered on his belt.

The other gunman reached his weapon, did some kind of sloppy ballet spin to face Bolan, then did a jerky little moon walk number as the Spectre's 9 mm hollowpoint rounds ripped into him from twenty feet. Falling, he managed one shot that seemed desperately loud inside the living room, his bullet taking out the giant TV with a crash that rivaled the gunshot.

So much for stealth.

The whole apartment might be soundproofed, but Bolan wasn't counting on it. In D.C., these days, a ton of money got you floor space. Privacy cost extra, and as far as keeping nosy neighbors in the dark about your business, you were on your own.

Bolan knew he had no time to waste. Two shooters down, and—

Crack!

The pistol shot came from his left and missed by some fraction of an inch. Bolan went low beneath the second shot and glimpsed the shooter, just retreating through a door into the kitchen. The Executioner's rounds were late, chewed drywall into tatters, but accomplished nothing else.

And if his rounds could penetrate the walls—

His adversary fired three more shots from the kitchen, hoping for a lucky hit, not aiming as he punched holes in the wall. One slug took out a hanging photograph. All three were high, confirming Bolan's prior experience that shooter's often overestimated targets they couldn't see.

He crept along behind the ragged line of holes and palmed one of his stun grenades. Now that the soft probe had been shot to hell, he might as well be quick and loud.

Reaching the door, he pulled the flash-bang's pin, gave the canister a sidearm pitch across the threshold, then curled up and waited for the blast. It came four seconds later, rattling the apartment walls and shattering all kinds of glass inside the stylish kitchen space. Bolan ducked in, went low beneath the pall of smoke and dust, to find an unexpected bloody scene.

The stunners were supposed to be nonlethal, but you always had to handle them with care. The way it looked, his enemy had seen the canister drop in and picked it up, hoping to toss it back at Bolan while he still had time. It had to have gone off in his hand, and not far from his startled face.

Not much was left of either, hand or face, when Bolan found the shooter. He was breathing, blowing scarlet bubbles through a nearly flattened nose, while blood pumped from the tattered ruin of his left hand. Bolan found his pistol in the corner, tossed it out into the hall beyond and left him to the task of dying on his own.

Three bedrooms left, and Bolan took them as they came. The first was empty, sheets and blankets rumpled as if Ulmalhama's bodyguards had just crawled out of bed to start their day.

Must be the maid's day off, Bolan thought. By the time he finished, they would need a whole construction crew.

The second bedroom, smaller than the first, was likewise empty, though in better order. Bolan wasted no time checking out the closets, looking underneath the bed. He knew the man in charge would have the master bedroom, and he hadn't seen it yet.

One door remained, right in front of him.

By now, his target had to know the hooker wasn't coming, had to have known that trouble had arrived. If he had any kind of weapons in his bedroom, there'd been time to reach them all and have them ready.

He shot off the bedroom doorknob and stitched a ragged figure eight of bullet holes into the shiny wood, from top to bottom. Bursting through behind that rain of fire, he dropped and rolled, fetched up against a chest of drawers.

Gunfire exploded from behind the bed, his quarry rapid-firing pistol shots, not taking time to aim. The bullets smashed a mirror, drilled a closet door, knocked divots in the wall.

How many left? Without a glimpse of Ulmalhama's weapon, Bolan couldn't safely guess. He had one chance, and even that could literally blow up in his face, if Ulmalhama kept his wits about him.

Bolan pulled another flash-bang from his belt but left its safety pin in place. He lobbed the canister left handed, saw it bounce once on the mattress, then drop out of sight.

How close to Ulmalhama's sweaty face? Would he be quick and smart enough to register the pin and know it wasn't armed? And if so, would he—

With a cry of panic, Nabi Ulmalhama vaulted from behind his bed, spraying the room with aimless pistol fire as he broke for the door. The Executioner was ready, waiting for him on the far side of the bed, and gutted him with half a dozen hollowpoint rounds below the belt.

The Saudi fell, gasping, convulsed with pain. His pistol

skittered off somewhere, across the hardwood floor. Blood pooled around his ruined lower body, while his legs thrashed uselessly, heels drumming.

Bolan knelt beside him, close enough to read the dying eyes while staying out of reach. Taking no chances, even now.

"Who…are…you?" Ulmalhama gasped.

"Nobody," Bolan answered. "Just a soldier paying off a debt."

"Is this…because…"

"The *Tropic Princess*," Bolan said. "And Bahia Matanzas. Are we on the same page, now?"

"I have…immunity."

"And how's that working for you?"

Ulmalhama's face twisted with rage, or maybe it was pain. He seemed about to say something, or maybe spit at Bolan, but his time ran out before the idea or the action could be realized. One instant, he was glaring hate at Bolan, then his eyes were blank and glassy. No one home.

"You got off easy," Bolan told the corpse, then put the killing rooms behind him, making for the stairs. It would be easy going, all downhill, and safer than the elevators. There was a back door, scouted in advance, that opened from the inside without setting off alarms.

He called Brognola from the car, knowing the big Fed would be awake. "All done," he said.

"No problems?"

"Not for me."

"We're square, then."

"Do you think so?"

"No," Brognola said, before he broke the link. "I guess not."

And they never would be. That was basic math. The Executioner had known it, going in.

The bad guys always started out ahead, and even if he wiped them out, the score was never settled. He could never make amends for all the damage done, the lives cut short or savagely disrupted.

They were never square.

The war went on.

Don Pendleton
SHADOW WAR

Intelligence has picked up chatter on the launch of an imminent strike of unknown origin and scope against the U.S., code-named Bellicose Dawn. Stony Man must navigate an unknown strike point, fragmented information and a brewing political firestorm. But soon they face the ultimate nightmare—men down, missing, maybe dead, and things going bad so fast that the day every Stony Man member prayed would never happen may have arrived.

STONY MAN®

*Available February
wherever books are sold.*

**Look for the 100th
Stony Man title in April with
a special collector's edition.**

TAKE 'EM FREE

2 action-packed novels plus a mystery bonus

NO RISK
NO OBLIGATION TO BUY

JAMES AXLER

DEATH LANDS®

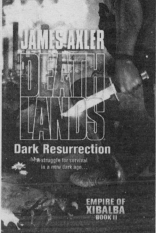

Dark Resurrection

Empire of Xibalba Book II

Captured by the pirate foot soldiers of the Lords of Death, Ryan Cawdor and his companions sail into a surreal world where blood terror reigns. In Mexico, Ryan is marked for slaughter. Helpless, Krysty, Dix and the others await a horrifying fate at the hands of whitecoats manipulating pre-dark plague warfare. As the Lords of Death unleash their demonic vision, hope—for Ryan, the others and civilization—appears irrevocably lost.

In the Deathlands, there's always something to fight for: one last chance.

Available March wherever you buy books.

POLAR QUEST
by AleX Archer

When archaeologist Annja Creed agrees to help
an old colleague on a dig in Antarctica, she wonders
what he's gotten her into. Her former associate has
found a necklace made of an unknown metal. He
claims it's over 40,000 years old—and that it might
not have earthly origins. As the pair conduct
their research, Annja soon
realizes she has more to
worry about than being
caught in snowslides.
With no one to trust
and someone out to kill
her, Annja has nowhere
to turn—and everything
to lose.

**Available January
wherever books are sold.**

Antarctica.
The land of snowslides,
alien artifacts and espionage.

GRA16

ROOM 59

THERE'S A FINE LINE BETWEEN DOING YOUR JOB—AND DOING THE RIGHT THING

After a snatch-and-grab mission on a quiet London street turns sour, new Room 59 operative David Southerland is branded a cowboy. While his quick thinking gained valuable intelligence, breaching procedure is a fatal mistake that can end a career—or a life. With his future on the line, he's tasked with a high-speed chase across London to locate a sexy thief with stolen global-security secrets that have more than one interested—and very dangerous—player in the game....

Look for

THE finish line

by

cliff RYDER

GOLD EAGLE®

Available January wherever books are sold.

www.readgoldeagle.blogspot.com

GRM595

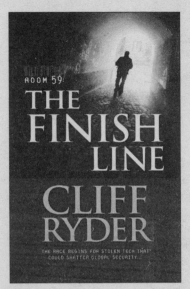

In January 2009

ROOM 59

**will have
a brand-new look!**

Same thrilling
stories, sleek
new packaging!

After a mission on a quiet London street turns sour, new Room 59 operative David Southerland is branded a cowboy. While his quick thinking gained valuable intelligence, breaching procedure was a fatal mistake. With his future on the line, he's tasked for a high-speed chase across London to locate a sexy thief with stolen global security secrets that have more than one interested—and very dangerous—player in the game....

Look for *The Finish Line,*
available January 2009
wherever books are sold.

**GOLD
EAGLE** ®